'Marvellously compelling and moving ... In short, pungent chapters — as intimate as pages torn from a diary, as bluntly cropped as photographs — the novel shuttles the reader between three cunningly interwoven stories ... Like the loves they describe, the sentences of the book are eccentric, disgracefully funny and shockingly beautiful by turns; determined both to describe the world as it really is and to invent it anew. Crane's death, in particular, is one of the finest things White has yet written ... When, as here, he is at the top of his form, White simply does it better than most'

Neil Bartlett, *Guardian*

'A novel clamorous with memorable characters'

Hephzibah Anderson, *Observer*

'As much as an account of sexual fascination, this is a novel about uneasy literary friendships. Among the many transplanted Americans visiting the Cranes is a vividly depicted Henry James ... the masterfully multi-layered *Hotel de Dream* is an illuminating commentary on storytelling and on the distance that separates life from fiction'

Ángel Gurría-Quintana, *Financial Times Magazine*

'White's imaginative recreations of Crane's work provide the novel's best passages ... marvellously convincing ... an engrossing book that memorably depicts gay life in an era when homosexuality was accommodated but never accepted'

Stephen Amidon, *Sunday Times*

'*Hotel de Dream* offers a touching depiction of romantic love'

Jon Barnes, *TLS*

'For nineteenth-century writers from Proust to Robert Louis Stevenson, the sickbed proved an enchanted realm of imaginative exploration. In the elegant, melancholy and spirited confection that is *Hotel de Dream*, Edmund White — and Stephen Crane — continue the tradition with grace'

Jane Shilling, *Sunday Telegraph*

'An elegant re-creation of the last days of the life of Stephen Crane'

Joyce Carol Oates, *TLS*

My Lives

The Married Man

Marcel Proust

The Farewell Symphony

Fanny: A Fiction

The Beautiful Room Is Empty

A Boy's Own Story

Nocturnes for the King of Naples

Skinned Alive

The Burning Library

Genet

Caracole

Forgetting Elena

States of Desire: Travels in Gay America

Our Paris

The Flaneur: A Stroll Through the Paradoxes of Paris

The Joy of Gay Sex (with Dr. Charles Silverstein)

Arts and Letters

HOTEL *de* DREAM

EDMUND WHITE

BLOOMSBURY

LONDON · BERLIN · NEW YORK

First published in Great Britain 2007
This paperback edition published 2008

Copyright © 2007 by Edmund White

The moral right of the author has been asserted

Bloomsbury Publishing Plc
36 Soho Square
London W1D 3QY

Bloomsbury Publishing, London, New York and Berlin

A CIP catalogue record for this book
is available from the British Library

ISBN 978 0 7475 9279 2
10 9 8 7 6 5 4 3 2 1

Printed in Great Britain by Clays Ltd, St Ives plc

www.bloomsbury.com

FSC
Mixed Sources
Product group from well-managed
forests and other controlled sources
Cert no. SGS-COC-2061
www.fsc.org
© 1996 Forest Stewardship Council

The paper this book is printed on is certified independently in accordance with the rules of the FSC.
It is ancient-forest friendly. The printer holds chain of custody.

TO PATRICK RYAN

My husband's brain is never at rest. He lives over everything in dreams and talks aloud constantly.

MRS. STEPHEN CRANE TO MORTON FREWEN
ON THE EVE OF CRANE'S DEATH

I cannot help vanishing, disappearing and dissolving. It is my foremost trait.

CRANE, IN A LETTER TO RIPLEY HITCHCOCK, 1896

At McClure's I met Stephen Crane the wonderful boy whose early work I saw and advocated in 1891–2. He is just returned from Havana and looked dingy and soaked with nicotine but appeared mentally alert and as full of odd thoughts as ever. He strikes me now as he did in early days as unwholesome physically—not a man of long life. He is now unusually careless in dress. . . . He was not overwhelmed with joy to see me. He looked yellow and his gaze was no longer frank. His attitude toward me had changed in some way.

HAMLIN GARLAND
DECEMBER 29, 1898

HOTEL DE DREAM

C ORA NEVER THOUGHT FOR A MOMENT THAT HER YOUNG husband could die. Other people—especially that expensive specialist who'd come down for the day from London and stuck his long nose into every corner of Brede Place and ended up charging her fifty pounds!—he'd whispered that Stevie's lungs were so bad and his body so thin and his fever so persistent that he must be close to the end. But then, contradicting himself, he'd said if another hemorrhage could be held off for three weeks he might improve.

It was true that she had had a shock the other day when she'd bathed Stephen from head to foot and looked at his body standing in the tub like a classroom skeleton. She'd had to hold him up with one hand while she washed him with the other. His skin was stretched taut against the kettledrum of his pelvis.

And hot—he was always hot and dry. He himself said he was "a dry twig on the edge of the bonfire."

"Get down, Tolstoi, don't bother him," Cora shouted at the tatterdemalion mutt. It slipped off its master's couch and trotted over to her, sporting its feathery tail high like a white standard trooped through the dirty ranks. She unconsciously snuggled her fingers under his silky ears and he blinked at the unexpected pleasure.

The newspapers kept running little items at the bottom of the page headlined, "Stephen Crane, the American Author, Very Ill." The next day they announced that the American author was improving. She'd been the little bird to drop that particular seed about improvement down their gullets.

Poor Stephen—she looked at his head as he gasped on the pillow. She knew that even in sleep his dream was full of deep, beautiful thoughts and not just book-learning! No, what a profound wisdom of the human heart he'd tapped into. And his thoughts were clothed in such beautiful raiments.

This little room above the massive front oak door was his study, where now he was wheezing, listless and half-asleep, on the daybed. The whole room smelled of dogs and mud. At one end, under the couch and Stephen's table, there lay a threadbare Persian carpet, pale and silky but discolored on one side with a large tea-stain the shape of Borneo. At the other end of the room it had amused Stephen to throw rushes on the floor as if he were a merry old soul living in crude, medieval splendor. There were reeds and rushes and grass everywhere downstairs, which confused two of the three dogs, Tolstoi and Spongie, into thinking they were outdoors: they weren't always mindful of their best housebroken comportment.

The maid, a superstitious old thing, had placed a small jar of tar under Stephen's bed. Did she think it would absorb the evil spirits, or hold off the ghosts that were supposed to haunt Brede Place?

Yes, Stephen had all the symptoms, what the doctors called the "diathesis," or *look* of consumption: nearly transparent skin, through which blue veins could be seen ticking, and a haggard face and a cavernous, wheezing chest. His hair was as lank and break-able as old lamp fringe. His voice was hoarse from so much cough-ing and sometimes he sounded as if he were an owl hooting in the innermost chamber of a deep cave. He complained of a buzzing in the ears and even temporary deafness, which terrified a "socialist" like him, the friendliest man on earth (it was Cora's companion, the blameless but dim Mrs. Ruedy, who had worked up this very special, facetious, meaning of *socialist*). Cora wondered idly if Mrs. Ruedy was back in America yet—another rat deserting the sinking ship.

Cora glimpsed something bright yellow and pushed back Stephen's shirt—oh! the doctor had painted the right side of his torso with iodine. At least they weren't blistering him. She remem-bered how one of the "girls" in her house, the Hotel de Dream, in Jacksonville, had had those hot jars applied to her back and bust in order to raise painful blisters, all to no avail. She'd already been a goner.

"Hey, Imogene," Stephen murmured, his pink-lidded eyes flut-tering open. He smiled, a faint echo of his usual playfulness. He liked to call her "Imogene Carter," the nom de plume she'd made up for herself when she was a war correspondent in Greece and which she still used for the gossip columns and fashion notes she sent to American newspapers.

"What is it, Stevie?" she asked, crouching beside him.

"Tell me," he said, "is the truth bitter as eaten fire?"

Oh, she thought. He's quoting himself. One of his poems. A kind of compliment, probably, since in the very next stanza, she recalled, there was something about his love living in his heart. Or maybe it was just idle chatter and all he wanted was something to say, something that would hold her there.

"I see," he said in so soft a whisper that she had to bend her ear closer to his lips, "I see you're airing your hair." He was making fun of her habit of loosening her long golden hair two or three hours every day and letting it flow over her shoulders. Arnold Bennett had been horrified, she'd been told, by her undressed hair when he dropped in unexpected for lunch one day. He'd told Mrs. Conrad (who'd unkindly passed the gossip along) that Cora's Greek sandals and her diaphanous chiton-like wrapper and loose hair made her look "horrible, like an actress at breakfast." But Mr. Bennett didn't have much hair nor would it ever have been his chief glory. There was nothing glorious about him except his prose, and that only intermittently.

No, Cora firmly believed that a woman must let her hair down every day for a spell if it were to remain vigorous and shiny (she'd heard that Sarah Bernhardt did the same; at sixty she looked thirty).

"Yes," Cora said. She was going to add, "We all need to breathe," but censored herself—that would be cruel to say to the gasping man.

Embarrassed, she blurted out, "We're going to Germany, Stephen." She hadn't intended on saying anything yet about her newest scheme to cure him, but now she had to continue. "To the Black Forest." She liked the sound of that, the name of her favorite cake—and also something solemn and shaded like the scene of a cruel fairy tale involving children and death by oven. "We've got to get you out of this damp country with its cold rains and harsh winds."

"Oh, Cora, Cora, I love the way you discourse," Stevie said, raising his finger to her cheek and touching its softness with something as dry and stiff as a gull's wing found on the beach after a long winter.

He indicated, with a shift of his eyes, the Sussex countryside just outside the window: green, peacefully rioting with wild-flowers.

"It's fair *now*," she said, "but if you want all four seasons, just stick around for a day."

She asked him about the trip to Germany. She knew he didn't usually like to discuss his failing health with her. She'd overheard him upbraiding someone for asking her hard questions about her future alone. "Don't upset Cora," Stevie had said. "It's a funny woman thing, but I think she likes me."

Now she told him how this German clinic was considered the best in the world. The same Dr. Koch who'd isolated the tubercu-losis germ ten or fifteen years ago was behind this clinic at Baden-weiler, which looked out on blooming fruit trees and stood on the edge of the Black Forest. After all, the Germans knew how to do these things, everyone else was an amateur.

Stevie echoed her very French pronunciation of *amateur*. She knew he liked to mock everything foreign in American expatriates, especially their linguistic affectations. The more Henry James fluted away like an English matron, the more Stevie when around him tried to sound like Daniel Boone or Andrew Jackson. Of course there was a serious concern buried under the tomfoolery; he was always so worried he'd forget the authentic American voice, that he'd start sounding like a limey, or like nothing at all. That was the worst: linguistic limbo.

TWO

THE LAST GOOD BOOK I WAS WRITING WAS THE ONE Hamlin Garland made me destroy. I wonder if I could write something now about my own life. I've never done that. What would I write? What would I say about myself?

I wish Cora would stop talking about my health. It's a jinx! Not that I really care what happens to me, I never wanted to live past thirty—but that's still two years away. . . . Keats and Byron: they got out young.

My mind is so full of money, twenty pounds here and fifty pounds there—of all the vast sums I owe and the meager payments I'm due—that I can't think of anything serious. Nor of anything frivolous, like this silly book, *The O'Ruddy.* I've got to dash it off. I suppose Cora will have the final installment on that if I die. Oh, I won't die, but Cora's blasted trip she's got planned for me to this miraculous German clinic could put me out of commission for a few months.

■ ■ ■

In Germany, is that where they practice pneumothorax? Is that what they call puncturing the lung and letting it deflate altogether?

These croakers have no idea what they're doing, not even the Germans. A bacillus, yes, but how to kill it? Their treatments all feel like fighting a horsefly with a slingshot. They want me to sleep in the great outdoors, even in winter, or, failing that, with my head sticking out the window. Or they want me to gorge on a second breakfast. Or repose on a sleeping porch, as if cold gales and ice crusting the water glass were ever a cure-all. No music, no sex, no conversation, except with dull old women, as if any form of stimulation were fatal. They're all charlatans. Somebody told me the other day—was it Wells?—that I'd never die from a hemorrhage, since he was coughing blood himself just a year ago. Of course he's always exercising on that bicycle with the giant wheel he devised, or pumping up and down on that lovely young wife of his, who's so under his spell she's changed her Christian name to suit him! Her name wasn't originally Jane but Amy. But Wells didn't like Amy. Damn good of him to say that to me, about my prospects; a fellow needs a bit of encouragement on some dim days.

If only Cora could locate her last husband and divorce him, I'd marry her (we tell everyone we're married but we're not) and she'd inherit all my future royalties, if there are to be any. And why not? *The Red Badge* is all right. Yes, I'm certain of that. It's still selling. People could never believe I hadn't seen a second of combat. The *Badge* was before my wars in Cuba, in Greece—well, when I did go to my wars they proved that the old *Badge* was all right. And my little whore novel, that's real enough to survive. Again, I wrote that before I became a reporter on the low-life beat.

I *have* written a few decent things recently. My yarn about the

Wild West was good: solid. But no, not much else. Most of it blather. Now critics are saying I never knew what I was doing, that the good things—*The Red Badge*, "The Open Boat," "The Bride Comes to Yellow Sky," "The Blue Hotel"—were just happy hits. Damn them! I took six weeks to write "The Blue Hotel." I had such a strong feeling that the Swede felt fated to die, that he was shaking in fear in anticipation of his death that very day, though in reality he had nothing or no one to fear, and in the end he was the one who provoked the violence. Even in Cora's newspaper columns I could always put in a good word or two—something fresh and queer. Most writing is self-dictating: yard goods. I was the only one of my generation to add a beat here and steal a note there. Rubato, it's called in music; Huneker told me that.

I'd written forty pages of my boy-whore book, Garland read them over and then with all his Wisconsin gravity in that steel-cutting voice he said, "These are the best pages you've ever written and if you don't tear them up, every last word, you'll never have a career." He handed the pages back to me and asked, "No copies? This is the one and only version?"

"This is the one and only," I said.

"Then you must cast it into that fire," he said, for we were sitting in a luxurious hotel lobby on Mercer Street, waiting for a friend to descend, and a little fire was burning just a yard away from our boots.

I couldn't help feeling that Hamlin *envied* me my pages. He'd never written anything so raw and new, so *modern*, and urban. No, he has his rolling periods and his yarns about his father playing the defeated pioneer farmer in the Dakotas, but he couldn't have written my pages. No, Hamlin with his lips so white they looked as if he'd kissed a snowman, all the whiter because wreathed by his wispy pale-brown beard and mustaches. His eyes sparkled with flint chips and he seemed so sure of himself. Of course I was writing about an abomination, though Elliott was just a kid, not a mildewed chump like Wilde—though you can find plenty of folks in England who knew him and would still defend him. We all hear them champion Wilde now, though no one stepped forward during the trial. Yeats was the only person who made sense when he talked about Wilde. Wilde's trial and the publication of *The Red Badge* occurred in the same year, 1895. But he represented an old Europe, vicious and stinking of putrefaction, whereas the *Badge* is a solid thing, trim and spare.

I threw my forty pages in the fire. It made me sick. A pearl worth more than all my tribe. And all through the lunch, with its oysters and baron of beef, I kept thinking the oysters were salty from my tears and the blood gathering in the silver serving dish—I thought that blood was my blood. I could barely eat and I couldn't follow the conversation with all its New York knowingness, reporter's shoptalk. Of course Hamlin hated my painted boy; he was even then scribbling his *Boy Life on the Prairie* in all its banal decency. Not that I'd ever dreamed of defending my little Elliott, but I knew his story was more poignant than scabrous.

God, I'm sounding absurd with my blood and tears and my resentment of old Ham. Hamlin was the one who gave me the fifteen dollars I'd needed to redeem the second half of *The Badge* from the typist. He was the one who had told me I was doing great things and got *Maggie* to William Dean Howells, and then Howells launched my career. Despite all the labels flying around in those days—I was supposed to be "an impressionist" and then there was Garland's "veritism" and Howells's "realism"—despite the commitment to the gritty truth, my truth, the truth about little Elliott, was too much for them to take on board.

Hamlin had been roundly criticized for saying in one of

his books that a conductor had stared at a female passenger "like a sex-maniac." That was enough to win him universal censure in America. No untoward deeds—just the word "sex-maniac," and next thing you know he was being compared to the sulfurous Zola himself. Oh, he's considered the devil's own disciple because his heroes sweat and do not wear socks and eat cold huckleberry pie . . .

The only one who could cope with my Elliott was that mad, heavy-drinking, fast-talking, know-everything Jim Huneker. Jim would drink seventeen beers in an evening out and feel nothing. He'd teach piano to an all-Negro class at the conservatory off Seventeenth Street and then retire to his boardinghouse where he was in love with a married woman named Josephine.

Her husband, a Polish merchant, never touched her, so Huneker said. He'd just stare enraptured at her V-shaped corsage and succumb to a red-faced paroxysm of secret onanism. Huneker seduced the unhappy lady just by touching her, the first time a man had touched those perfect breasts. But he was a busy one—he once gave a dinner for all three of his ex-wives. He had a long, straight Roman nose he was so proud of that he liked to speak in profile, which could be disconcerting. His very black crinkly hair sat on his white brow like a bad wig, but he made me pull on it once to prove to myself it was real.

Huneker was such a womanizer! I could write about him in a memoir, couldn't I? As a music critic he'd encouraged aspiring female singers to prejudice his reviews in their favor through what he called "horizontal methods." Huneker also had a quasi-scientific interest in inversion. Usually he'd scorn it. He condemned *Leaves of Grass* as the "Bible of the third sex." Initially he was hostile to the eccentric, effeminate pianist Vladimir de Pachmann; he feared that Pachmann's silly shenanigans onstage might damage the reputation of serious musicians before the usual audience of American philistines. Pachmann would stop a concert to say to a woman in the front row, "Madam, you're beating your fan in two-thirds time and I'm playing in seventh-eighths." Or for no good reason he'd interrupt his playing to pull his hoard of diamonds out of his pocket and sift them from one hand to another. Because of these hijinx Huneker called him "the Chopinzee," and they traded insults at Luchow's when they first met and poured steins of beer over each other's head. But a year later they mellowed and Pachmann came to dinner and played for Huneker for five hours, till three in the morning.

Tchaikovsky also troubled Huneker for his indifference toward women. Huneker was particularly disturbed by the story that seconds after Tchaikovsky met Saint-Saëns, the composer of *Samson and Delilah*, they were both in women's clothes dancing the tarantella. When Tchaikovsky died, Huneker said he was "the most interesting if not the greatest composer of his day"; Huneker also defended Wilde and said the English were silly to abhor him after they'd courted him for years.

I was with Huneker one wintry day walking up the Bowery. We'd just had lunch at the old Mouquin's down at Fulton Market and we were strolling along in one of those brisk winds that drive ice needles through your face even in the pallisaded fastness of Manhattan. In spite of our sole meunière and red velvet banquette we were suffering from the elements. Sometimes weeks go by in New York and I scarcely notice if it's hot or cold, fair or cloudy—and then a stinky-hot day floats the reek of the tenements upstream, or the gods decide to dump four feet of snow on the nation's busiest metropolis. And then the snow turns it into a creaking New England village.

The weak sunlight was filtering down through the rail slats of the overhead elevated tracks and every few minutes another train rumbled slowly past above our heads like a heavy hand on the keyboard. Beside us horses wearing blinkers were pulling carts down the center of our street between the El tracks. Their shaggy forms and pluming breath were scarcely visible through the blizzard of sideways snow. The dingy-white awnings on every building were bulging above the sidewalks under the weight of snow. The poor prostitutes in their scanty clothes were tapping with their nails on the windowpanes, trying to attract a bit of custom. One sad girl, all ribs and scrawny neck, huddled in a doorway and threw open her coat to show me her frozen wares. Huneker with his three plump wives and horizontal sopranos certainly couldn't bother even to sniff at these skinny desperadoes through his long Roman nose. We walked and walked until we decided we had had enough of the wind's icy tattooing of our faces. We were about to step into the Everett House on Fourth Avenue and Seventeenth Street to warm up.

Standing in the doorway was a slight youth with a thin face and dark violet eyes set close together and nearly crossed. He couldn't have been more than fifteen but he already had circles under his eyes. He smiled and revealed small, bad teeth, each sculpted by decay into something individual. He stepped toward us, and naturally we thought he was begging, but then I saw his face was painted—carmined lips and kohled eyes (the dark circles I'd noticed were just mascara smudged by the snow).

The boy stumbled and I caught his cold little hand in my bony paw. His eyes swam and floated up into his head; he fainted. Now

I'm as frail as he was, but back then I was fit. I carried him into the Everett House.

He weighed so little that I wonder if he filled out his jacket and trousers with newspapers to keep warm, or to appear less skinny. There was the faint smell of a cheap woman's perfume about him and, because of the way I was holding him, the stink of dirty, oily hair that had absorbed cigarette smoke the night before.

I was ashamed of myself for feeling embarrassed about carrying this queer little boy tart into a hotel of well-fed, loud-talking men. All of them were illuminated by Mr. Edison's new hundred-bulb chandelier. The doorman took a step toward us, so agitated that the gold fringe of his epaulets was all atremble; he held up a white glove. Idiotically I said, "Don't worry, he's with me," and good old Huneker, who's a familiar face there, said, "Good God, man, the boy's fainted and we're going to get some hot soup down him. That's what he needs, hot soup. Order us some hot soup!" Huneker went on insisting on the soup as if it answered all questions about propriety.

There was a table free but the headwaiter glanced at the manager—but he couldn't stop us. We headed right for the table, which was near Siberia, close to the swinging kitchen doors. I placed my frail burden in a chair and, just to bluff my way out of being intimidated I snapped my fingers and ordered some hot soup and a cup of tea. The headwaiter played with his huge menus like a fan dancer before he finally acquiesced and extended them to us. Slowly the businessmen at the other tables gave up gawking and returned to their conversations. Maybe that is why I was so sympathetic to Elliott, as I soon learned was his name. I'd had to carry him through a sea of disapproval.

Now that I looked at his painted face I feared I might vomit. Huneker was studying me and smiling almost satirically, as if he knew my discomfort might make a good story that very evening, when Josephine, she of the V-shaped corsage, held court. "Stephen pretends to be so worldly," I imagined he'd soon be saying, "but he is the son of a Methodist minister and a temperance-worker mother and he *did* grow up in darkest New Jersey, and though he's fraternized with hordes of daughters of joy he'd never seen a little ganymede butt-boy buggaree before, and poor Stephen—you should've seen his face, he nearly vomited just as the headwaiter was confiding, 'The joint won't be served till five.' "

Let him laugh. That was another thing I liked about Elliott: the boy became devoted to me, though ultimately I was unable to save him.

ORA RETURNED WITH THE TEA THINGS AND FOUND Stephen awake and feverish with excitement. His great mustaches, which for months had been drooping, unclipped and uneven, now seemed to be bristling with electricity. His eyes were sparkling and looked as if they were about to emerge out of his haggard, narrow face.

"Cora," he whispered, "I want to dictate something to you."

"Oh, yes, my love, we must get on with *The O'Ruddy*. If we can finish another ten thousand words we might get another installment of fifty pounds from Mr. Pinker. There's a bailiff about to issue a warrant for my arrest in London, and the butcher of Brede won't deliver another joint until we've paid him off. He made the worst row this morning, and the kitchen help cast reproachful looks at me, as if poverty were a character flaw. Those two nurses cost every week two pounds four shillings and sixpence each—and that Dr. MacLaughlin ran us fifty pounds. Of course he was so encouraging his visit was a good investment, but I took matters in my own hands and got the necessary fifty pounds out of Lippincott by writing their London representative, Mr. Garneson, and just saying outright, 'I don't think they will hesitate as it was a matter of saving Stephen Crane's life.' That got them going, you can bet! After all, Stephen Crane *is* a national treasure."

Cora rattled on, talking about this home industry of hers called Stephen Crane, but he was floating up somewhere near the cornice and drifting down through the long, slanted rays of sunlight coming through the dirty window.

Now she was on to something else. She was gossiping about her recent trip to Paris with Stephen's niece and how the women there were wearing green, nothing but green. His mind skipped ahead and suddenly she was saying the news of his health was competing with the Boer War and the American presidential campaign for the headlines. Absurd, but Cora liked to exaggerate. He could never tell how famous he was, how either over- or underestimated his celebrity was. It seemed that most of the people he met had never heard of him unless they were other writers, though he was prepared to believe, as Cora had put it tactlessly, that he was more famous than his books.

They had plans to travel to Napoleon's final place of exile and death, the island of St. Helena, somewhere between Brazil and Africa, because there was an English prison there where Boer prisoners were jailed, far from English laws and English eyes. They could torture the enemy there and get away with it, exact confessions from them, and never have to submit to a civic or military tribunal. Stephen was supposed to write about the Boer question for the New York *Journal*—but St. Helena was twelve hundred miles away and now he thought the trip would have to wait. He wondered if the English were torturing the Boers just for the pleasure of it. Cora said the sea air would do him good.

Maybe he was dying after all since he couldn't much care about the deaths of Boers or that women in Paris were wearing green. Cora was pacing up and down the room, thrashing her skirt with his riding crop, but even the sight of the crop didn't make him want to go out riding. Even when he'd hemorrhaged the day after Christmas, he'd loved riding across the Sussex hills as far as Rye and Henry James's house; he'd half-believed that by posting in his saddle and swallowing great gulps of cold air he could some-how "freeze" the disease and not permit it to grow. Maybe even Mr. James's slippery, deviant conversation was curative.

He fell asleep and dreamed of galloping overland with Elliott but the saddle hurt him dreadfully and he woke and realized the pain was coming from his anal fistula. For the last two weeks he'd endured the most awful pain whenever he tried to shit, or even sit up. Wells, that "touchy, perverse little artist" as James described him, had tried to laugh off the fistula as well, pointing out that none other than Louis XIV had had the same malady and had suc-cessfully subjected it to *la grande opération*. Dozens of courtiers at Versailles pretended to have the same disease and underwent the same surgery, just for the copycat prestige of it all. Crane had laughed—but even that hurt him.

Cora watched him dozing off. The minute the fire went out of his eyes his face was ashen, the white silky ash that a breath can blow off the top of a dead log. She wanted to have Stevie moved down-stairs to the room next to the front door so that he could stagger out to a chaise longue in the garden on fair days (or, more realisti-cally, fair hours, given this climate). He'd always been thin and his ribs had always been sharp enough to scrub a shirt on, but now his

face was so sunken that his teeth stood out under his cheeks like a
fist under a sheet. He was sweating. Every day for an hour or two
he'd sweat with a recurrence of his Havana fever.

The thought of Havana made her remember how he'd hidden in
that city for three or four months, away from her, away from everyone. They'd already been through so much together—their encounter in Florida on December 4, 1896, the war in Greece they'd
both covered as reporters, life in England. He'd left for Cuba in
the spring of 1898. In the fall he went to ground—she'd heard
nothing from him for three months. He was living in Havana.
She'd been frantic for news of him—and for money! Morton had
just leased her this house, Brede Place, and she'd had all the ex-
pense of moving down to Sussex and of picking up a few sticks
of passable furniture and hiring a staff—but she had no money,
Stevie was hiding! He said he loved her and dreamed of marrying
her but he'd disappeared. Now she had her doubts—did he really
love her?

He'd coughed blood during the last days of the Spanish-
American War and had been quarantined for typhoid on a ship
bound for Key West. But he'd always seemed to have enough energy for another assignment. To him, it was like digging spurs in an
old horse's flanks, he said. He'd jumped ship and sped off to Ponce
for the three-week war in Puerto Rico.

But after that, he'd sneaked back to Havana and filed stories
from that old, sinful, rotting city. There were only four gunboats
in the harbor and the wreck of the cruiser *Alfonso XII*, stripped of
its engines and guns. His fever and shakes and sweat seemed natural enough in streets that stank of rotting guavas and open privies.
He could still write, but his hand was so shaky some of his words

were illegible. He had been stabbed in the hand by that mad Cuban in a dance hall. Cora had seen one of his handwritten letters, but it wasn't to her.

Why had he dropped her?

He'd made her suffer terribly. She'd even cabled Secretary of War Alger, demanding news of Crane. She'd tried to track him down at the Hotel Pasaje in Havana, but he'd vanished. Alger never responded. Later, much later, she'd learned that the *Journal* had cut off his expenses since he hadn't been delivering the articles—and the Pasaje was the best and costliest hotel in town. She'd been frantic with jealousy, convinced that Stevie was living with a younger, prettier woman. She'd sent letters through William Randolph Hearst himself, but Stevie didn't answer. She'd rented Brede Place and had *no money*! Even to eat, much less pay something on her tradesman's bills.

Then she'd thought she must sail for Havana and save Stevie from his señorita temptress, whoever she might be.

Stevie had disappeared on September 6th, when he was forced to leave the Pasaje, till October 4th, when he finally sent Cora a cable. What was he doing all that time? She supposed he was nursing his wounded hand, which had become infected, but why had he abandoned her? He made no effort to write back. Nor was he writing journalism—maybe a few poems.

Cora knew that he thought he'd thrown away his talent to support her immoderate *train-train*, but they were both to blame. She'd spent years and years icing champagne and lighting Cuban cigars for male customers at the Hotel de Dream (named after its previous owner, Mrs. Dreme, though Cora had spruced up the spelling). Naturally she'd wanted to entertain over here in England. Their Christmas pageant, "The Ghost," had been the sensation of the whole county, the villagers had all swooned with delight and even the vicar, though pleading a cold, had transmitted his greetings. James, Conrad, Wells, and of course Stevie had all had a hand in the proceedings. Never had such a silly play been written by so many geniuses. There had to be gifts for friends and drinks for everyone. Stevie had drunk himself sick; the extravaganza had prompted his hemorrhage.

Some people criticized her for traveling to Paris with Stevie's niece when he was ill and in need of nursing, but her articles on fashion, which she'd sold to a dozen American newspapers, were a major source of their income now—and besides, Steve had promised his brother, the judge, that his daughter would see all the major sights in Europe and how else would they've known about "the phenomenon of green"?

FOUR

NOW HE AWAKENED AND FOR A MOMENT HE WAS STILL IN the bright environs of his dream—New York on a busy, sunny day, a building going up on every corner, the clangor of cast-iron beams being hammered into place, the greased roar of the El pivoting overhead, the hollow staccato of horse's hooves dragging big-wheeled wood carts dangerously close to each other. A yellow cable car was sliding past, the sun dazzling off its windows. Women were rushing by, the breeze fingering the feathers in their hats, their practiced hands lifting their skirts to negotiate the muddy curb. Everyone was talking at once, or crying out their wares, selling things from pushcarts. It was an unexpectedly hot day in his dream and the men and women appeared to be steaming in their wool clothes and many layers. In the dream there were no children. That was odd: no children. And then, beside him, smiling up at him, was Elliott, a distinct person in his own right but somehow part of him as well, as if they shared something crucial—a spine or a lung, say.

After he'd met Elliott on that cold day in front of the Everett

House, they'd sat at the table so long that eventually the joint was wheeled past in its silver cart: the roast beef, the lamb with its mint sauce, the goose with its apple sauce, the boiled corned beef and cabbage, and the boiled leg of mutton.

It sickened Elliott even to look at it, but I ordered him a plate of white meat of chicken, no skin and no sauce, as well of a dish of mashed potatoes, no butter. He was so weak I had to feed him myself.

"Are you ill, Elliott?" I asked him.

"Yes, sir."

"You don't need to 'sir' me. I'm Stevie."

Elliott's eyes swam up through milky seas of incomprehension—this man with the jaunty hat and scuffed shoes and big brown overcoat wanted to be called Stevie! Elliott whispered the name as if trying out a blasphemy.

"Tell me, Elliott—what's wrong with you? Do you think you have consumption?"

Elliott blinked, "Pardon?"

"Phthisis? Tuberculosis?"

More blinking.

Huneker butted in and said, "Good God, boy, bad lungs? Are you a lunger?"

Elliott (in a small voice): I don't think so, sir.

Me: Fever in the afternoon? Persistent cough? Sudden weight loss? Blood in the sputum?

I laughed. "You can see I know all the symptoms. If you are in the incipient stage, you must live mostly outdoors, no matter what the season, eat at least five times a day, drink milk, but not from tubercular cows—"

Huneker: Are you mad? The boy is a beggar so of course he

lives outdoors, but not in nature but in this filthy metropolis! And he'd be lucky to eat a single meal a day.

Tell me, boy—

Me: His name is Elliott.

Huneker: Far too grand a name for a street arab, I'd say. Tell me, Elliott, when did you eat last?

Elliott: Yesterday I had a cup of coffee and a biscuit.

Huneker (scorning him): That a nice, generous *man* gave you, upon arising?

Elliott (simply): Yes.

After Huneker rushed off, babbling about his usual cultural schedule, all Huysmans and Wagner, a silence settled over the boy and me. We were between shifts of waiters and diners and the windows were already dark though it was only five-fifteen on a cold, rainy Thursday night in November. We breathed deep. The warmth of the hotel's luxurious heating had finally reached Elliott. He relaxed and let his coat fall open. He was wearing a girl's silk shirt, dirty pink ruffles under his blue-hued whiskerless chin.

He smiled and closed his coat again. We chitchatted about one thing and another and I told him a few new jokes and he laughed. He even tried to tell me a joke but it was pathetic, a little kid's joke. It was obvious that he'd been too weak even to talk, but now, with some food in his stomach, he became voluble.

He told me he hadn't spoken in his normal boy's voice for weeks and weeks. "Usually we're all shrieking and hissing like whores."

Me: And saying what?

He: If you want to say someone is *like that* you say, at least *we* say, "she"—and of course we really mean *he*—"she's *un peu* Marjorie."

I laughed so hard he didn't know whether to be pleased or offended since to laugh at someone's joke turned him into a per-
former, a figure of fun, and Elliott didn't see himself that way.

He said the perverse youngsters he knew called themselves
Nancy boys or Mary Anns. Automatically I pulled out my little
black reporter's notebook and moved the elastic to one side and
began to take notes. The boys would accost men at a big rowdy
saloon on the Bowery they called Paresis Hall and ask, in shrill
feminine voices, "Would you like a nice man, my love? I can be
rough or I can be bitch. Want a rollantino up your bottom? Is that
what you are, a brownie queen? Want me to brown you? Or do you
want to be the man? Ooh la la, she thinks she's a man—well, she
could die with the secret!"

As for his health I divined from all the symptoms he was describing that he had syphilis and the next day I arranged for him to
see a specialist and follow a cure (I had to borrow the money—
fifty dollars, a minor fortune). I had to convince him that he
needed to take care or he'd be dead by thirty. Though that threat
frightened him no more than it did me. I expected to be dead by
thirty or thirty-two—maybe that was why I was so fearless in battle. He seemed as weary of life as I was; we both imagined we'd
been alive for a century already and we laughed over it.

I said, "Isn't it strange? How grown-ups are always talking
about how life speeds by but it doesn't? In fact it just *lumbers* along
so slowly." I realized that by referring to grown-ups I was turning
myself into a big kid for his benefit.

He said, "Maybe time seems so slow to you because you look
so young and people go on and on treating you in the same way."

I was astounded by this curiously mature observation—and
chagrined by the first hint of flirtation. He was flirting with me.

I told him that I'd lost five brothers and sisters before I'd been born, which left me just eight. That made Elliott laugh, which he did behind his hand, as if he were ashamed of his smile.

"I'm the youngest of four, all brothers," he said. "My mama died when I was three—she and the baby both. We lived on a farm fifty miles beyond Utica. When I was just a little thing my daddy started using me like I was a girl."

"He did?" I asked. I didn't want my startled question to scare him off his story. "Tell me more."

"And then my brothers—well, two of the three—joined in, especially when they'd all been drinking, jumping me, not in front of each other but secretly, in the barn after their chores, or in the room I shared with my next-older brother, the one who let me be. My daddy had been the county amateur boxing champion thirty years ago and he was still real rough. Almost anything could make him mad."

"Give me an example," I said.

"Well, if the breadbox warn't closed proper and the outer slice had turned hard—don't you know, he'd start kicking furniture around. We didn't have two sticks stuck together because the two oldest boys took after him, and they'd flash out and swear something powerful and start kicking and throwing things. The only dishes we kept after Mama died were the tin ones, and they were badly dented. Things sorta held together when Mama was around and we sat down to meals, at least to dinner at noon, and she made us boys go to church with her, though Daddy would never go. Then when she died, we stopped seeing other folks except at school, but us kids missed two days out of three. Daddy could write enough to sign his name and said he saw no rhyme nor reason in book-larning for a field hand. I liked school and if I coulda went more regular I might've made a scholar, but Daddy liked us home, close to him, specially me since I fed the chickens and milked all four cows and tried to keep the house straight and a soup on the boil, but Daddy always found fault with me, in particklar late at night when he'd been drinking and then he'd strap my bottom and use me like a girl and some days my ass, begging your pardon, hurt so much I couldn't sit still at school without crying. The teacher, Miss Stephens, thought something might be wrong, 'cause I had a black eye, sometime, or a split lip, and once she pushed my sleeve back and saw the burns where Daddy had played with me."

By this point we were walking up Broadway toward Thirtieth Street, where I lived with five other male friends in a chaotic but amusing bear's den of bohemian camaraderie. I hoped none of them would see me with the painted boy. The rain was beginning to freeze and the pavement was treacherous. I steered Elliott into a hat shop and bought him a newspaper boy's cap, which he held in his hands and looked at so long that I had to order him to put it on.

The more Elliott talked the sadder I felt. His voice, which had at first been either embarrassed or hushed or suddenly strident with a whore's hard shriek, now had wandered back into something as flat as a farmer's fields. He was eager to tell me everything, and that I was taking notes, far from making him self-conscious, pleased him. He counted for something and his story as well. I sensed that he'd guessed his young life might make a good story but he hadn't told it yet. There was nothing rehearsed about his tale, but if he hesitated now he didn't pause from fear of shocking me but only because till now he'd never turned so many details into a plot. He had to convert all those separate instances and events into habits ("My daddy *would* get drunk and beat me"). He had to supply motives ("He *never* had no way of holding his anger in") and paradoxes ("I guess I loved him, yeah I guess I did, and still do, but I don't rightly know why").

He slipped on the ice at one point and he grabbed my arm, but after another block I realized he was still clinging to me and walking as a woman would beside her man and I shook him off. As I did it I made a point of saying something especially friendly to him; I wanted him to recognize I was his friend but not his man. I felt he was a wonderful new source of information about the city and its lower depths, but I drew back with a powerful instinct toward health away from his frail, diseased frame. I couldn't rid myself of the idea that he wasn't just another boy but somehow a she-male, a member of the third sex, and that he'd never pitch a ball in the open field or with a lazy wave hail a friend fishing on the other shore. The whole sweet insouciance of a natural boy's mindless summer was irrevocably lost to him.

Of course I'd had a difficult childhood, too. I'd not had an easy time of it.

Nor had my mother. I was her fourteenth child and she was forty-five years old when I came along. The four babies born before me all died just after birth. As I told Elliott, my father, the Reverend Jonathan Townley Crane, was dead by the time I was seven or eight and my mother when I was twenty; the poor woman was worn out by childbirth and the struggle to stop other people from drinking. She was a good mother—she'd arranged for me to do my first bit of journalism at Asbury Park.

But if we were poor and I was passed from one older sister to another, nevertheless no one beat me and I had strong but loving women to feed me and shelter me. I was sent to a private school, and later, in college, first at Lafayette and then at Syracuse, I was such a good baseball player (catcher, then briefly shortstop, then catcher again) that after school people said I could get a job on a professional team, even though I was just five foot six and weighed only 125 pounds. Now I weigh even less—in fact I've made no headway at all since I was twelve.

I invented words, I read Flaubert and Tolstoy, I fell in love with brainy virgins, I satirized middle-class beach life at Asbury Park, and at every step I was surrounded by bemused and tolerant relatives and friends. I could afford to smoke my pipe, let my hair grow long, sweep about in a borrowed ulster and lose the buttons on my shirt, which never had a clean collar, all because my brother Edward was impeccable and my father had been irreproachable. I was the bohemian exception.

My hunger was real enough and often in New York I could only afford to breakfast on potato salad, the cheapest item at the nearest delicatessen, or I had to dine on chestnuts, which I roasted in a candle flame. But I could always get a good meal if I went to Port Jervis and the house of my brother the judge. My childhood was just the opposite of Elliott's, whose father buggered him thrice a week from age six on, who was supposed to cook and clean and work as the family squaw-man. No sports, no friends—and the worst of it was that he had to keep a big secret. He had to tell no one about the bruises and lash traces, about his brothers and father taking turns. All his mental energy went into a dull, repetitious prayer: I mustn't tell, I mustn't tell, I mustn't tell. In a musical score, Huneker told me, when one measure is repeated several times without a change, the shorthand mark is a slant with a dot on either side. Elliott's thoughts could be scored that way.

At a corner I said goodnight to Elliott and told him to meet me the next day at three beside the statue of Washington in Union Square. I promised I'd make a doctor's appointment for him (he had a chancre) and go with him; what I didn't tell him was that I wouldn't trust him with money since he might spend it frivolously (no more than now I'd trust myself or Cora with it). I had no idea where he went that night or slept but at least he'd eaten a hot meal, which I'd been able to pay for only because I'd just sold a story on street life to the *New York Press*.

That night I tried out a mention of my new encounter on one of my friends, Corwin Linson, but he who always laughed at my adventures (the bearded lady, the Siberian twins, the Negress of Hoyt Avenue) grew strangely silent when I revealed I'd met a painted *boy*. He was an artist who'd studied in Paris with Gérôme and whom I thought of as terribly worldly (he was seven years older than I). He did that portrait of me in profile in which I'm all cheekbones and pasted-down Napoleonic spit curls; the first time we'd met he told me I resembled Napoleon "but less *hard*," to which I murmured, "I would hope so." We called him "CK," maybe because "Corwin Knapp Linson" was a mouthful.

He'd laughed and laughed when I'd advised Armistead Borland to stick to Negro women if "they're yellow and young," though I meant it perfectly seriously. But now he wasn't laughing. He squirmed out of his chair and added a red dot to the canvas on the easel. I'd brought up a subject that would embarrass any man, no matter how wild and anarchist he might be. Which made me feel alone and understand how lonely and defiant Elliott must be (I refused to call him "Ellen," as he wanted me to).

Why could I tolerate him? Or rather why did he appeal to me, to my innermost being? Why was I the only normal man who could see how wounded he was? My Cuban battle pieces will be called "Wounds in the Rain," and that could serve as the name of Elliott's portrait in words, something fluid and vague and painful. Maybe I responded to him because we were both ill. I had a hacking cough even then and a kid's face; he and I both looked like sick waifs. And then maybe he appealed to me because he was a whore—after all, I always felt good around prostitutes and they bring out something gallant in me. Christ, my own wife is a whore and a whoremonger. That's one way to escape the curse of a Methodist upbringing.

But there was also something hard-eyed and disabused about Elliott that touched me. I suppose there's nothing more appealing than a small person who is in obvious pain but unreachable. Whose child's heart is still alive, still beating inside a block of ice. I had the strong impression that I could look through the ice to see it, trailing its veins and arteries, pulsing not with contractions but with light.

I was as poor as Elliott in those days. I lived from hand to mouth. I was always borrowing a quarter from CK, who could earn as much as four dollars for an illustration and had a facile pen and brush. CK would just slip me the quarter surreptitiously, as if we were thieves palming off stolen goods, even when no one else was around. Our parody of embarrassment concealed a real embarrassment about borrowing and lending. Not that I lent him anything often. I can still remember one morning when he asked me for a quarter. "Hey, mister," he whispered, still playing our game, "got two bits for a jay down on his luck?" To my chagrin, I had not a penny and just rushed out, confused. I said, "Not a red, Ted. Not even for a jay, CK."

I lived in different places but stayed some of the time with CK on Thirtieth Street and Broadway. Or I stayed at the old Art Students League. At the League a small square door opened onto the street and led into airless, sunless hallways that melted improbably one into another in a slumberous procession. The art students had moved out, leaving behind vast empty studios with rain-smeared skylights, scarred walls, and tilting floors. On the ground floor tailors and plumbers and tinkers had taken over the shops, and now they were moving up and requisitioning the abandoned studios. Soon the whole building would be a beehive of commerce.

CK shared his studio with an artist who painted expensive sets of dinner dishes (three cherries for the bread dish, two ripe peaches and hazy Concord grapes for the charger, an apple or cherries on the bread plate—I watched him work hour after hour). There were three cots set up with dirty bedclothes half pulled aside to reveal broken-backed mattresses sweated through to resemble relief maps of an eroded landscape. The air was thick with smoke, especially when all our friends (the "Indians," as I called them) gathered for a few hours on a Saturday evening, the one time we were all free.

Everyone teased me for sitting the whole time with a lit but unsmoked cigarette smoldering between my yellow-stained fingers. They teased me about everything—my rumpled clothes, my fascination with women in red dresses, my sentimental verses, my banjo playing, my rapacious way of grabbing a magazine or book to pluck it clean of quaint phrases or queer facts and then cast it aside, for I was too impatient (and too chary of being influenced) ever to finish a book. I thought of myself as an aesthete, or rather a sensibility in ragged trousers, and I didn't want to learn or acknowledge or appreciate. No, I just wanted to be *jostled* by language as one might be shouldered aside by pedestrians scurrying up Broadway.

That was the noisiest corner in New York. The fire engines would rush past in a clatter of gongs and hooves. Late at night, when the theater around the corner let out, megaphones shouted out for carriages. Between midnight and four only the occasional slow horse clip-clopped past. Toward dawn milk cans were shoved off wagons and banged against restaurant delivery doors, where they were rolled slowly inside by sleepy sous-chefs. Then everyone was suddenly awake and shoes struck the pavement and wagons jostled for space; giant wheels scraped against the curb. Everyone was talking at once. New York had released its ten thousand devils.

I would lie on the divan and doze and listen to the roaring megaphones and the military rumor of booted feet marching home and always the voices murmuring or laughing. Around ten at night everyone seemed to be drunk and the men were roaring out songs though they couldn't remember the words and women were laughing their unnatural-sounding shrieks just to excite their escorts—and it seemed everyone was going to end up very soon making love or some half-hard approximation of it.

FIVE

H ENRY JAMES HAD COME TO VISIT. HE'D SENT A NOTE FIRST and Cora had torn it open and skimmed it as she rushed to do something else, and then she had had to sit down and parse it.

Chers Enfants—Since I will be in the vicinity of Brede for reasons I will not deprive you the pleasure of divining, I will "drop by" toward teatime in response to your extremely kind "open" invitation (the openness of which can constitute an ambiguous ouverture d'esprit one sometimes cowers before).

À bientôt—your Oncle d'Amérique in lavished affection if not in fact in wealth.

She found the grammar hard to diagram mentally and the quotation marks embracing ordinary words somewhat ominous. Teatime? Good heavens, he'd be here in a moment! Why did he write such beardless sentences?

She found Lucy in the blackened medieval kitchen holding dishes under the trickle of sink water and humming fiercely. "Do we have any cake to serve Mr. James?" Cora asked.

"Lord, madam, is that old woman coming to bother us again with his hemming and hawing?"

Cora started giggling. "Can you help me put my hair up? I've been airing it only half an hour but Mr. James will be shocked to see it down."

Lucy dried her cold red hands on her dirty apron and accompanied Cora to her dressing table, the one that sat at an angle on its spindly legs and caught only a glimmer of cold blue light in its tarnished mirror. Once Lucy's hands warmed up they went about their work with agility.

When she rose from doing her "*beauté*" Cora looked out the oriel window and spied Mr. James on his bicycle approaching the house. "Oh, God," she mumbled as she almost simultaneously clapped a smile to her lips. She hurried to the great oak door just as Mr. James was removing the bicycle clips from his trousers and straightening the plaid leg. He lifted his soft brown hat as if in greeting but it was only to pass a large white handkerchief over his shiny skull. He tilted his head to one side in response to Cora's high birdcalls of greeting.

A bright, droll smile cracked open the tragic mask of his face. A sort of rumbling of language began in his feet and shivered up his legs, shook his torso, and finally spilled from his throat in a high, nasal stammer: "There was—and undoubtedly still *is*—a mist on the hills that I find—*er*—" and here he paused and stuttered as he sought the mot juste, his eyes wandering as if the word itself were a butterfly drifting from the small-leaved boxwood bush into the smoky vastness of the hall. "That I find—*er*—"

"Picturesque?" Cora asked brightly.

But Mr. James instantly pushed the offensive banality aside and at last spat out: "*Damn* picturesque."

The words so painfully chosen plunged him into an iridescent play of irony and pleasure, which swirled over his features and ended in a firm thrusting forward of his shaved jaw.

As Cora followed him upstairs to Stevie's studio the great man stopped suddenly and nearly knocked her over. He stood there one step above her, and asked her minutely detailed questions about arrangements for Stevie's care and her plans to take him to Germany and the Black Forest. His questions implied she needed supervision. At every point he would start his infernal rumbling in search of the right word as if he were an espresso pot—a purely egotistical exercise, she thought, since she dared say he had no respect for her opinion. In any event she was always quite happy with the slipshod approximations of ordinary human conversation. Nor did he like her. She knew that James had reportedly told someone after she first met him that she was a "bi-roxide" blonde considerably older than her husband, with a dull common manner and a past. And he'd claim that initially he'd taken her to be a servant. Come to think of it, maybe it was Richard Harding Davis who made that crack about her hair color.

The minute he saw Stevie on his daybed Mr. James lit up and trundled his solid, portly body to his side, though typically he couldn't summon up the usual effusions. Rather, he looked back at her and then again at Stevie and at last he said, with a strangely episcopal opening of his hands, palms up, "And here is Cora and here is Stevie." Then, because he could never say anything just once, he added, "And here is Stevie." And he settled on the straw-seated wood chair with an abruptness that made her fear he'd crash through the bottom.

Stevie seemed happy, though he'd just awakened from a deep, feverish sleep. As though to distract his visitor from his own disorientation he asked in a boy's clear voice, "Tell me, why do you live here?"

Mr. James appeared startled, he who usually barraged his friends with questions but was of such an extreme discretion that he almost never submitted to their interrogations, which in any case were invariably fruitless. But now he said, *"Here,* in Sussex?"

Stevie nodded.

James said, "I like golfers. I like seeing them strolling about in their plus-fours."

He and Stevie laughed at the silliness of it all.

"If you mean in England," the older man continued, "I've always been half-English, since I spent so much of my boyhood reading *Punch.* But if I'm half-English, I'm also half-French, since when I'm in a rush I jot notes to myself in French."

He ended his remarks with an odd drum roll of his hand on the side table. Nothing this man came up with, Cora thought, was foreseeable, neither his words nor his deeds. At her place of business in Florida, the Hotel de Dream, she'd never entertained his sort. "Not the sort of individual we'd get," she thought dismissively.

She could tell by the way that James lit up around her husband that he was queer as a football bat. At first she thought it was just due to how English and prissy he'd become, but her friend the late, dear disabused Harold Frederic, another transplanted American writer, had set her straight: "He's all woman and he wants everyone to treat him like a pope—or the Queen Henrietta Maria."

But Mr. James never gave in to his impulses—he wouldn't hug or kiss the poor, thin sweating Stevie. No, he would study him and prod him, then slather him with praise in a sentence that might end with a sting in its tail.

"Mr. James," she said, "did you know I've invented a canteen filter?"

The great man looked at her wild-eyed; he liked to be prepared for any turn the talk might take but she left him nonplussed once again. "A-a-a-a what?"

"When we were covering the war in Greece I realized how hard it was for soldiers to find pure water—water that wouldn't give them dysentery. You know, poor Stevie was crippled with it, he barely got off the pot fifteen minutes to actually witness the wretched war—and so I've come up with an invention, it's going to make my fortune, it's a filter fixed right inside the canteen that removes all impurities. It only needs to be cleaned once a week. Would you like to see the maquette I've had fabricated? I'm collaborating with an engineer, Mr. Fredrick Bowen, I'd never be able to go it alone. He's made three models and has separated mud from water. He says he's uncovered important facts about metallic and carbon content."

Henry James's face registered his growing horror at everything she was conjuring up: leaking bowels, money, mud, war, and the unspeakable manufactured item itself. His mouth twitched and his eyes tightened in small spasms, as if unheard explosions were being detonated far inside the cavern of his mammoth head. At last, recognizing that she'd become an immense and immovable detour, he lifted his hands above his head. He appeared to be warding off a downpour of pebbles.

Cora liked shocking him. She saw that he didn't know what to make of her bright, breezy manner. Maybe he found her filter to be irrelevant to the grand, deathbed scene with Stevie he was preparing. A fife to the full orchestra that was raising its hushed, murmuring chorus. She didn't give a damn. She needed to live, to survive, and what means did she have beyond the filter and the pages Stevie kept grinding out? The money would go into the trip to Germany she was planning, she needed every penny for the journey. She said to James, whose upraised hands were only now very slowly wilting back to his lap, "What about it? Wanna see the filter?"

"I can't," Mr. James said, "extract everything I need to from what you just uttered, but if I scurry off with it like some great *nut* in my pouch you can be sure that later when I'm alone I will, er, *extract* something to your advantage."

"It's all very simple," Cora said to this man whose feelings she was sure were as undiluted as hers but whose thoughts were so infernally dirty and roiled.

"I'm going to need money, lots of it, when we take the train to Dover on May seventh—that's just next week come to think of it—and make our way to the Continent. We'll need our own railway carriage and a doctor and a nurse or two to travel with us."

Mr. James blinked rhythmically under the successive blows of Cora's words. She knew he hated the red stinging hand of fact slapping him back and forth in the face.

"We'll stop in Dover for a few days until Stevie has all his energy back. We'll stay at the Lord Warden Hotel, which Mr. Conrad tells me is just off the Admiralty Pier, where steamers depart for Calais and Ostend three times a day. Of course we'll take our dog Spongie, too, but I'd wager the whole shebang will cost up to a hundred pounds, everything rounded off to the nearest zero."

Mr. James's sensitive, stony face had been willed into impassivity, but it still flinched under the rapid blows of "Spongie," "shebang," and "nearest zero." In an orthographical aside to himself he wondered if it were spelled "chebang." He'd seen it written once like that in Mark Twain.

Suddenly he remembered something and brought out of his pocket a dog-eared copy of a magazine. "I have a story in here," Mr. James said, fixing Stevie with a scowl. "I've dedicated it to you.

I think"—and here he broke off for rhetorical effect—"I *think* it will be of special interest to you."

Cora didn't mind it when other men "mashed" on Stevie. Nor other women. She knew he was famous and young and so sweet and sincere that he was irresistible. His fame worked into the equation because it constituted something like a bold-printed finger stamped in red in the margin to draw the reader's attention to a remarkable passage.

Stevie was soft-spoken and frail and really insignificant physically except for his eyes, the irises the color of wet sand, their soulfulness enhanced by his flowing mustaches in an oddly romantic reciprocity she'd noticed in other young men. Stevie went to some pains to shave that little groove between the septum of his nose and the top of his upper lip. The *philtrum* it was called; Stevie had taught her that, he who loved strange words.

She didn't mind that other people admired her little husband and even lusted after him. In her work at the bordello she'd observed the hydraulics of desire so often that she didn't take pleasure too seriously. Some men could mistake lust for love—but she felt that Stevie in any case wouldn't lust after this pudgy bald man, though he loved Mr. James's conversation (she could smell James's lemony eau de cologne now that his body was heating up as he rumbled along in conversation).

She left the men and went to her own room to work on the text for her next article.

She thought how different they were, Mr. James and Stevie. James never did anything or went anywhere and had no hobbies; all he did was write and contemplate life as obscured by the prismatic interference of the mirrors in his mind. Stevie was a fellow of action. He was fearless in war, as everyone said, and he liked to drink and woo the ladies. Their New Year's Eve party, three months before, had shown in the twentieth century with a three-day orgy.

The quantities of drink and food all consumed by the light of hundreds of candles had made James say that Stevie had the manners of a Mile End Roader, by which he meant a poor, foul-mouthed cockney. For decades Mr. James had been acquiring English polish and had beat them at their own game, whereas here was Stevie, earning the exorbitant sum of fifty dollars per thousand words, writing methodically in his tiny script on long sheets of foolscap to pay for these routs. Stevie thought he was the Baron of Brede with the dogs snapping at bones under the table amongst the rushes and the guests throwing bread down from the minstrels' gallery, thereby setting off massive food fights—here was little Stevie, as pale as old ivory, laughing so hard he wept, the little prince admidst his rowdy courtiers. And Mr. James disapproved of anyone taking England and its traditions so lightly, as if it were all available just as an amusing motive to be sounded on an out-of-tune spinet, something as inconsequential and nourishing as air.

And then Mr. James couldn't write good clear prose like Stevie. James had thought about his art for half a century and devoted all his life force to it, but Stevie laughed at it all, would never be caught saying a word about "art," shrugged and pled ignorance if the subject came up, flutily imitated Mr. James, though Stevie's New Jersey accent kept any parody from succeeding.

And yet Stevie was the great American stylist. He had no critical chatter, no culture, though he'd thumbed carelessly through Anatole France and George Gissing. But he got it all.

Oh, Stevie, she thought. How she loved his bantam arrogance, that hard, nagging core of primary masculinity that kept throbbing inside him—an assertiveness that Mr. James would never know and could approximate only through a eunuch's sly attitudinizing. Stevie was a man even in his exhausted state. She loved his profile, the way his upper lip protruded out, his ear as intricate as a cross-section of a fetus, his eyes as flat and sandy as a shark's, his cheekbones high as a Mohawk's. She loved the timbre of his nasal voice—the knowing tone of someone who always got the joke and caught the reference.

Not that he was a scoffer. He appreciated all these great writers they were meeting—James and Conrad especially, Wells and Gissing—and enjoyed their acceptance and admiration. He was their equal and treated as such, whereas back in America he would have to pay homage to men who were his inferiors, William Dean Howells and that cultured chatterbox Huneker.

She was the reason Stevie was living in England, even though its climate was so bad for his lungs. In puritanical America people knew about her past, whereas here in England they were out of range and those who did know didn't care or were compromised themselves—Ford Madox Hueffer and Wells and Harold Frederic all had divorced or separated and Lord knew Henry James was what her Florida girls called a "morphrodite," by which they probably meant a "hermaphrodite."

After Mr. James left, Cora went back to Stevie's room. She asked to see the copy of the *Anglo-American Review* containing James's short story. She wondered why James thought the story would be of special interest to Crane.

"May I have it?"

She wanted her husband to give it to her, not just lend it, since she felt it might contain some veiled, super-subtle attack on her that Stevie would surely be able to decode.

With his usual acuteness and generosity Stevie understood right away how anxious it made her. "Here," he said, "I'm going to make you a present of it." He wrote:

These pages were given by Henry James to Stephen Crane
and by him to
Mrs. Stephen Crane
Brede Place
Sussex
England.

Cora suddenly had tears in her eyes as if someone had handed back a sheaf of blackmailer's letters.

"Don't you want to read it?"

"You can just give me the gist—"

Which suddenly struck them both as so funny that they laughed, astonished. Precisely because Henrietta Maria's stories always lacked "gist."

Back in her room she read "The Great Condition," which as best she could make out through the smokescreen of prose told the story of an American widow with a past. A rich young Englishman wants to marry her even though she has no fortune, but will do so only if she can swear there was no scandalous moment during her life in the Sandwich Islands (Where?! unable to picture them on the map).

The American widow tells him she will confide the whole truth to him but only six months after he marries her (the slyboots, Cora thinks, admiringly). But the young man, Braddle, keeps wondering if there might not be "some chapter in the book difficult to read aloud—some unlikely page she'd like to tear out."

In the end Braddle hurtles off to the Sandwich Islands and the widow marries his best friend, a man so in love with her he doesn't trouble her with suspicions about her past. At last Braddle comes back from his international inquest and admits he can find absolutely no traces of scandal. He's lost the prize, Mrs. Dameral, and all because he was troubled by something as elusive as honor.

Cora stiffened. She stood and paced the room thrashing her skirt impatiently with the crop. She'd been nagged and nibbled by the queer strategies of James's language: "We live in beguiled suppositions," he'd written, "without the dreadful fatal too much," a phrase that had left her stumbling forward: "Too much *what*?" "Is there anything 'off' about her?" Braddle had asked. Of Mrs. Dameral: "The charming woman was not altogether so young as Braddle, which was doubtless a note to his embarrassment."

Was Stevie embarrassed that she, Cora, was a few years older? No, he liked it. He liked sleeping with his head on her breasts (that was one way for a man to be younger) or playing the spoiled tyrant as he reared above her and plunged in (that was the other way). And of course he enjoyed reversing their ages and making her suck on his thumb as if she were the baby; he'd even tried to feed her with his hard, brown, minuscule nipple, which had brought her scant benefit.

Outside her window, the light hung on breathlessly in an endless English evening. She thought the farmers nearby must have eaten their suppers and were longing for bed. But still the horses stood in the fields, shifting their weight occasionally as they grew bigger and darker and flatter as dusk fell.

She hated Mr. James's story, for though it ended innocently enough, it was designed to trouble Stevie. It took place in England, the woman was older and American, guiltless though every line suggested that a past was a deplorable thing for a woman to have. Cora took out her sewing scissors and cut out the pages and threw them on the grate where a feeble, blue fire flashed orange and ate them with mindless greed, before circling and settling back down to doze.

SIX

WHEN MR. JAMES GAVE ME HIS STORY IN THAT FLIMSY year-old magazine and dedicated it to me, I realized how much he lives for his writing. I know that I, too, can still write something good—something that would even impress the Master.

I remembered that the next day, the afternoon after I'd first encountered Elliott, I accompanied the boy to the doctor. We'd met as arranged by the statue of Washington in Union Square and then walked over to a general practitioner who had an office near the Bureau of Surgical Relief for the Outdoor Poor at the foot of East Twenty-sixth Street. A Dr. Murray, I recall.

Today Elliott wore no makeup or perfume, though on closer inspection I could see he'd drawn a black line under each eye. "That's a bit rough," I said and made Elliott thoroughly wash his face in the lavatory of a nearby saloon.

"Gee, you'll make a bad impression on the doctor, he could even have you locked up. You know they think that's a responsible thing to do, to imprison syphilitic whores, keep them from spreading their muck to decent folk. Since you've got it on your pecker, he'll assume some girl slopped it your way. Best let him think that."

I mitigated the harshness of my words with a wink. I wanted to be stern with Elliott and yet a friend as well.

Around suppertime I slipped away to amble the streets. At that period I was writing my scenes of everyday life—the column about an Italian man who falls down in the street with an epileptic attack, or the one about a bakery catching on fire and a policeman summoning the fire wagons. I'd described the noise and lights and glamour of the fire patrol wagon before I'd identified it—an example of my impressionism: ". . . a storm of horses, machinery, men. And now they were coming in clamor and riot of hoofs and wheels, while over all rang the piercing cry of the gong, tocsin-like, a noise of barbaric fights." In the same way I evoked the firefighters before naming them, "There was shine of lanterns, of helmets, of rubber coats, of the bright, strong trappings of the horses."

I wanted to publish a piece on a diseased whore's visit to the doctor, but even if I turned Elliott into a female I knew my editor would never buy such a piece, nor could he. But I wanted to describe how afraid of the venereal ill—and disdainful of them— the doctors are. No hospitals will accept them and few physicians. When we went to his office, the doctor unceremoniously made Elliott strip and lie down on a plain white slab. He spread Elliott's legs and touched his penis and testicles with his hand sheathed in a glove. He kept up a stream of unseemly jocularity. It was all over in a minute and a half. No microscope, no culture ovens, no hot running water.

Twice the doctor bathed his own fingers in eau de cologne (without removing the glove) and rubbed the moisture through his beard. He lit a Bunsen burner as if it would disinfect the air. Of course all he could come up with as a treatment was the usual mercury, which induces salivation—and spit, according to Galen, is the humor that is in excess. A pitiable business, medicine, which hasn't improved since ancient Rome. Dr. Murray mumbled something about the disease being highly contagious when it was "florid"—neither Elliott nor I, we discovered later, knew what that meant. "Flowers?" I said. "Aren't flowers florid?"

Elliott shrugged.

When we joined up later I was cold and exhausted and had a coughing fit. Elliott waited patiently for me to catch my breath. He drew me down to a park bench beside him in Madison Square. Finally the coughs subsided and I said, "What a fine pair we are, you with the syph, me a lunger!"

We both laughed a small, troubled laugh because it wasn't very funny and my words spelled my doom.

Elliott said, "If you're so interested in the low life you should let me give you a tour of the fairy saloons."

I agreed and we set off, the air thick with the sound of hooves and voices and the perpetual ding-ding-ding of the trolleys. Almost as if all these noises were the snow inside the globe someone had shaken, a blinding sonic storm.

The sky was heavy with clouds except down toward Wall Street, and from a clearing there a cold evening light radiated, as if the south were west. The various buildings rose to different heights without any plan and in a bewildering range of styles, all like weeds competing in a forgotten garden: one a frilly fern, and the next a sharp blade of grass; neoclassical columns too wide and squat, as if groaning under an excessive weight; baroque balconies proudly sporting pregnant, uninscribed cartouches; a French Renaissance château with fake chimneys and a steeply mansarded roof and senseless ornamentation, flung like freckles on a farmer's face—all designed, if you will, to house a wax museum!

In the streets every man was wearing a bowler except me in my slouch hat and Elliott in his newsboy's cap. Lights were springing to life in gold effusion around us, a soft breeze was ruffling the awnings at nearly every window like heavy lids drooping in sleep. The names of firms, half-erased by the gathering dark, spoke a Babel of languages: Pinaud, Gottschalk, Ruggiero, and a late, horse-drawn truck proclaiming: "Henry Adam Pianos and Furniture."

We reached Bleecker Street and headed west until we arrived at a façade like any other. "This is the Slide, where you'll meet my sisters and mothers"—he looked sideways at me with his quiet, farmboy's smile—"you know, other fairies, young and old."

"Oh," I said, shrugging, "for a moment I thought you meant real women and I got my hopes up."

"Oh, love," he said, already acting a part, "don't get it up, not out here in the cold, you might freeze it off!"

He wasn't very good at his act but I cuffed him anyway.

When we entered the saloon, at first it seemed like any other, with a long, carved wood bar on the left, bottles of liquor on glass shelves, a huge mirror behind the bar reflecting and somehow improving the faces of the weary men sitting on high stools. Bits of ham and cheese which looked pawed over were on a greasy platter. A harsh light emanated from the gas lamps. It was still early and there were only a few men here, and farther back a table of women sipping steins of beer.

"Those aren't women," Elliott told me, with a slight air of superiority.

I looked closer and realized the hands around the mugs were

big and ropey, though the nails were painted. The faces wore clownishly bright makeup but the noses were too large, the bones too prominent, and the—yes, the telltale Adam's apple.

"Oh look, Ducky," one of them croaked. "You may approach the Sublime Porte."

Elliott whispered pedantically, "That means we can visit them."

We edged closer—absurdly I took off my hat and held it in my hands, and so did Elliott, as if we were domestics before the quality.

"What have you drugged in, Miss Pussy?" the same transvestite demanded of Elliott.

"He's *all* normal," Elliott said, grinning sheepishly.

"Hmmn, normal, perhaps, but obviously questing," the creature replied. He raised an absurd lorgnette, heavy with rhinestones, and examined me through it. "Not a very sturdy-looking normal. Just one more feeble little normal normaling about. Bit like a drowned rat, your Mr. Normal, if you ask me. But he is a perfect heartface. You tell me he isn't in the life?"

"Oh, no, Your Majesty, he's pure man."

"Ooh, he doesn't half look feminine, don't he?"

Another denizen of the table weighed in with a chorus of "Fairies will make your thumbs prick," and everyone cackled.

"He's not a fairy," a third man boomed in a deep voice through slick red lips. "Look at the color of his eyes!"

Suddenly everyone stared at my crotch (Elliott whispered, "Eyes is a secret rhyme for size, the size of your unit").

The lorgnette was aimed at my flies. The first man asked, "What you got in there, the Rockingham tea service?"

Now the singer was singing again but this time was chanting, "My heart starts a racket every time I see your packet," which made them all fall about and not so much laugh as *mime* laughing—literally holding their sides or pitching forward like hand puppets shaking all over and hanging down below the edge of the proscenium.

"That's no tea service," the basso profundo said, "that's a demitasse spoon."

"Ooh, you'll frighten her off, our Miss Man"—jerking his head toward me (I was obviously "Miss Man"). Then back to the other transvestite: "You're a wicked old queen! An evil fairy! Pure Carabosse!"

"I'm not Carrie Boston!" he replied, "I'm the empress of Astonia and your name is—Miss Bird E. Bath!"

I thought they were funny but I felt apprehensive as I always do with professional comedians. Would they be able to sustain it? Then I tried to picture these ladies in their ordinary male garments at their usual jobs. Perhaps the Empress was a butcher with an old wife back home in Brooklyn and four dirty-faced children. Under that one's elbow-length puce gloves might be tattoos from navy days. Though he's wearing a floor-length skirt he's spread his legs under it in a most unladylike way. And this guy is probably Italian, with a hairy chest and gold crucifix under his blouse and cameo.

"And what does Miss Man do, Lovey? I hope she's not down on her luck like your usual clientele."

"He's a journalist," Elliott said proudly.

Once pronounced, the word *journalist* set off a chorus of alarmed shrieks and a fluttering of fans and a panicked rolling of eyes. "Is Miss Man going to write about us and get us closed down or gawked at by sightseeing normals—or is she going to attract Lily Law? The orderly daughters? Tell us, purge, purge, purge!"

"He means the police," Elliott interpreted, though I felt he was himself just one step ahead of me. "Sometimes the cops are called flymen. Or Betty Bracelets." He put his wrists together to suggest handcuffs.

"Ladies, ladies," I said, making repressive gestures like a conductor trying to hush the strings, "don't worry. It would be impossible to write about you without shocking my morning readers so much they'd choke on their toast." Their hysteria and dress-up somehow tranquilized me. I felt I was in charge and they were crazed, fluttering things.

"Well, Sweetums, remember: royalty don't like exposure," the basso profundo said.

"Exposure, Your Nastiness?" the Empress chimed in. "You're not thinking about exposing yourself again? Though it must be said we'd all need a jeweler's lens to register the effect if you did expose yourself."

"Heartface," the third lady said, touching my sleeve, "what about a round of beer? A pint and a half of ale for the three of us?"

"Their Majesties don't seem to understand," I said, "that their faithful servant is thundering broke."

A new chorus of tut-tuts burst forth.

"Not the sort of admirer we had in mind for you—and, Lovey—" they said to Elliott, "not a proper suitor for an embarrassed miss such as you. *Financially* embarrassed!" They shrieked.

Eventually I was introduced to the Countess of Upper Silesia and Her Grace the Dowager Marchioness of Baden-Baden ("Nothing graceful about her, Pussy, but she do be double-*b* bad," said the Empress). As we clowned around I found my mind wandering to Alice in Wonderland and the White Queen and the Mad Hatter. My new friends had an "off-with-their-heads" peremptoriness and a frazzled impatience with earthbound life.

Did these creatures wear these clothes on the street? How had it first occurred to them to dress up? Elliott had mentioned they were prostitutes, but who would find them desirable? And wouldn't their scorn wither any man's pride?

I grew tired of standing and I was racked by a siege of coughing.

"Not a well woman, our Miss Man," said the Empress with the put-on cockney accent of an old harridan. When I recovered, a weird moment of silence descended over us and all that could be heard was the hissing of gas jets, and all that could be smelled was the odor of rice powder and stale beer. A moment crept by. Then a second one. I could see a drop of sweat snaking down the Countess's face and eating through an inch of white lard. I wondered if these ladies sat or stood to pee.

Elliott pointed to the rickety-looking stairs leading up on the right and left to a shadowy balcony. "Later on there will be fairies seated up there, waiting for customers, but it's too early for them now."

"Why aren't you dressed as a woman?"

Elliott said that he was a "flame-fairy, which means I wear boys' clothes and girls' makeup—there are men that prefer that." He announced this taxonomic nicety as if he were teaching me something basic about the world.

"Bold! But Miss Man is bold with her questions, our Miss-Man-girl-reporter," shrieked the Countess. "I just know she's going to write us up, though I'm far too proper a gal to have my name before the public. Me mum will be having a hissy fit."

"Mais oui, chérie," boomed Her Grace with the remnants of a dockworker's drone, "show him the inner sanctum and invite him to disclose the secret life of the hierophants to the great unwashed." She made a loose gesture up toward the balcony.

Upstairs were round tables covered with soiled clothes and

candles like a dirty solar system. "They're not terribly interesting," I whispered to Elliott.

Elliott looked alarmed. "They're not?"

It was as if he'd offered his mother's diamonds for sale as a last resort and been told they were paste. Poor Elliott—he'd run away from his terrible farm and arrived penniless and friendless in this big, sooty city and somehow, miraculously, found these glamorous, older friends who shared his vice and were so frightfully clever. He knew they might offend ordinary folks but till now he'd never doubted that they were fascinating. He looked shattered and I immediately regretted my words.

"You're too good for them, Elliott," I said. "They've become hardened and deformed. They're not real people, neither fish nor fowl."

"Oh, they're foul enough, Lovey," Elliott whispered with a crooked smile; his reply defended the Royals, in substance and style.

As we left the saloon, I noticed a man in a bowler standing on the other side of the street, staring at us, or rather at Elliott. His ungloved hands, as big and white as boiled hams, hung down at his side. He was wearing a velvet-collared Chesterfield which he'd thrown open as if to breathe more easily, or to cool off, though it was a cold night.

His face would have looked beseeching if it weren't so resigned. Maybe because I'm so short I notice men's height—he was easily over six feet tall but appeared to regret it.

"Do you know that man?" I asked Elliott.

"Yes," he said, "I know him. He's in love with me."

SEVEN

CRANE COULDN'T GET THE IMAGE OF THE MAN OUT OF HIS mind as he lay in the Lord Warden Hotel and watched the curtains billow in the cool sea wind. He remembered how that man—Theodore Koch—had unnerved him, as if he were a bankrupt standing on a bridge over a rushing river.

The train trip to Dover had exhausted Crane. They'd traveled with their servant, Richard Heather, with good, flustered Dr. Skinner, with the two nurses, Charlotte Gardner and Annie Taylor, with Crane's niece Helen and dear old Spongie, who turned out to be such a homebody he did nothing but growl softly in the back of his throat like an old man who complains all the time about new faces and unfamiliar food.

They decided to stay in the hotel as long as it took for Crane to regain the force necessary to travel to Calais, which was a scant thirty miles across the Channel. Crane couldn't leave his hotel bed but he claimed that if he looked out the window he was indirectly aware of the glare of the chalk cliffs falling on the water, almost as if a pale sun were rising under the waves. He liked the sound of gulls shrieking as they circled the ferries pulling toward the Admiralty Pier down below.

He knew they had no economies set aside and that Charlotte and Annie had been sent out to live on sandwiches and that Cora wasn't eating at all. She always looked impeccable in her bronze-colored silk blouse with the high collar which was just a shade darker than her lustrous piled-up hair. One evening when he fretted about money she told him that Morton Frewen had lent her a hundred pounds—but he knew she was lying.

Conrad came to visit him in the late afternoon. As it happened, Stevie had dictated to Cora, just before leaving Brede Place, a letter to Arnold Bennett, asking him to get Conrad a pension on the civil list: "He is poor and a gentleman and proud." Crane might have been describing himself. Crane added that he feared no one might ever like Conrad's books beyond a cult of other writers. Stevie was deeply embarrassed when he discovered that Lady Churchill was circulating a letter asking "the friends of Stephen Crane" to contribute to an emergency fund. In any event, Lady Churchill was unable to raise any money for him.

Conrad was as small as Stevie but he bristled with energy. His eyes were pinpoints of trouble, his mouth a flat line of pain, his shoulders so strong and high that he appeared to have no neck at all. He entered the room as if he'd just been asked to ascend a throne and, after an initial reluctance, now meant to show just how decisive he could be. The tips of his waxed, black mustaches and spade-shaped black beard preceded him. His skin was sallow and the lines in his face spoke of long night watches on the ship of art.

He sat beside Stevie and planted both hands on the sick man's shoulders. "My dear friend," he said, his breath smelling of tobacco and sardines, "I can see you're about to leave this world."

Crane smiled at his frankness. "True, but don't let Cora hear you. She's not ready for the inevitable." This sentence, which he recognized was cogent and well-formed, and which he was proud to have pronounced, exhausted him. "Anyway, only one lung is in trouble. The other is sound."

Conrad told him that he had had a breakdown ten years earlier, after he'd come back from the Belgian Congo. "I went to a clinic at Champel in Switzerland. I got over my depression—just as your Black Forest clinic will no doubt cure you."

"Why did you have a breakdown?" Stevie asked.

"I heard about terrible things up the Congo—there'd been a certain James Slago Jameson who paid the natives six handkerchiefs for the privilege of watching—and sketching!—a slave girl sacrificed and eaten by cannibals. Jameson was a scientist with little glasses; he treated it all as research."

Stevie looked up into Conrad's eyes, which frightened him with their impersonality, an eagle's eyes, attuned rather than revealing: he gave nothing away. His conversation was similar. Like James, he asked detailed questions but gave not even the vaguest answers.

Wickedly, Wells had pointed out that Conrad thought the silent *e* in *these* and *those* should be voiced, which he did with such authority that for an instant one questioned one's own accent. Now Conrad said, "You are here-uh, with these-uh gulls and those-uh masts—everything needed for a voyage, even a voyage into the infinite-uh."

Soon, like all writers everywhere, they were talking about money. But Conrad could never tolerate chitchat for long, not even shoptalk, and he quickly changed the conversation to his own work. He'd recently written *Youth*, which had been inspired by Stevie's "The Open Boat," and *Heart of Darkness*, which reflected his own misadventures in the Congo. There he'd seen horrors perpetrated by the Belgians that he never forgot, and there his own health had been seriously undermined. Now he'd begun *Lord Jim,* which also betrayed Stevie's influence, and he spoke at some length of his plans for the book.

Cora came in with tea and cakes for the two men, though Crane never touched the food or drink. Cora said, "And Mr. Conrad, how is your son Borys?"

Conrad smiled, which counted as a decided unbending, given his starchy manner. "We spent a day last week with Henry James. Mr. James held Borys on his lap for a solid half-hour against the child's will. You know what a fidget he is, but with Mr. James he seemed to recognize a superior being who mustn't be vexed. Finally Mr. James put him down with a kiss. Borys ran to me and whispered, 'Poppa dear, isn't he an elegant fowl?' I'd been reading him Lear's *Book of Nonsense* and now he says things like that."

After Cora withdrew, Crane whispered, "Tell me, JC, have you ever known any inverts?"

Conrad's face stiffened. "Of course as a sailor I *heard* about such abominations. Why on earth do you ask?"

"I'm thinking of writing about a boy prostitute I interviewed once in New York."

Conrad groomed his beard and mustaches for a few moments with his pale hand. At last he said, "I'm afraid it would offend people so much you'd have trouble getting it published. Ever since poor Wilde's trial, society has grown even less tolerant."

"Well, Wilde," Stevie said. "Anyway, a crime against nature was only one of his sins. He was also a dreadful cad."

Conrad looked blank. "A—what?"

"Cad," Stevie repeated.

For a moment he wondered if his American accent were the problem. Should it be pronounced "cod"?

"I've never heard that word," Conrad said. Even after Stevie spelled it, Conrad shook his head and Stevie realized that Conrad's literary English, so strangely fluent and nuanced and menacing on the page, was an act of the will and no guarantee of conversational ease.

"Of course you're right," Stevie said, "but the subject interests me—not even the subject, but this particular youth, Elliott. I once wrote forty pages about him and destroyed them, but now that I'm at the end and have nothing to fear . . ."

He was too tired to complete the thought. When he awakened much later in a cold sweat, Conrad was gone. The sky outside was clouding over and someone had closed the window. He could just about remember Conrad saying something to the effect that physical pain and dissolution should not lead a writer toward vice. Stevie now wrote a sentence in Cora's journal: "I will write for one man only and that man is myself."

That evening he had a clear head and he dictated to Cora for half an hour.

THE PAINTED BOY

Elliott found himself in the New York train station. Men in bowler hats and good wool overcoats were plunging past him in the weak sunlight that filtered down through skylights. He was a farm boy and had never heard so many voices at once, or seen so many shoes. He couldn't look up into their faces.

He sat on a wood bench polished smooth by human contact, the wood armrest dark from the acids in human hands. He looked down long tunnels of striped light, the stepped-in rising skylights that covered a mile's length of rail and spanned ten tracks, each with its own platform.

He had no plan. His daddy had beat him hard a week ago, and Elliott had resolved he'd run away after the welts healed. He didn't know why but he wanted to offer a pure body to New York. It was the only thing he had to give.

A man with fancily sculpted facial hair and a brown suit the color of turned earth was slumped back on a bench across the way, looking funny at Elliott. A smile flickered across his lips. Eventually he came over and sat next to the boy.

"Waiting for your parents to pick you up?"

"No, sir, I ain't got no one here in New York City." Elliott tried to speak clearly and honestly and not to mumble. He knew he had a bad habit of mumbling—the schoolmarm had told him so. He wondered if this man were some sort of policeman: Had his father already set the authorities on his trail?

"I'll bet you're waiting on a family friend."

Elliott was tempted to nod, but what if this man was an authority who would catch him in his lie? Or what if he was just an idler who could outwait him and discover his shameful secret: He knew no one and had nowhere to go.

"Well, my Aunt Mauve might come, so she said, I mean . . ."

The man didn't seem capable of sitting upright. He kept sliding down the bench until his trousers were stretched taut across his crotch—and then he had to pluck at them and sit back up before the sliding process began all over again.

The tracks were entirely housed in glass. The clouds raced across them, and the sunlight picked out a dusty carriage far away as if a magic wand had just ignited this one and not all the others.

Elliott had taken a year to put together the one-way fare from upstate New York and his village into the Grand Central Depot. He had no plans but he felt that someone, somewhere would help him in this city. He admired how all these passing men could afford draped trousers, polished shoes. He envied them their jobs where he guessed they sat around at desks all dressed up and frowned and then smiled and spoke in quiet voices.

"Here as a visitor or hoping to stay?" the man asked. "By the way, I'm Silas. I'm called Silas Aspen."

They shook hands.

"I'm Elliott, and I'm hoping to stay."

"Well, you know, there are many jobs for newcomers. You could be a peddler of sponges, or a peddler of pretzels. You could be a bootblack or push an ash cart or a rag cart or shovel snow. They're laying cable for the new cable cars."

All these jobs sounded daunting and improbable to Elliott, who had only two bits left in his pocket and no friends, unless Silas Aspen could be counted as one.

Silas edged a bit closer but slid down farther in his seat before he said, "Maybe you'd like to be a newsboy. I could fix you up for that."

"That would be wonderful. What do I do?"

"I'll fix you up. Don't worry."

They shook hands again. Elliott was so relieved that he liked the way the man's skin felt dry and hot.

They ambled out onto the Forty-second Street. Elliott was intrigued by the shadows cast on women wearing bonnets by the elevated trains passing overhead. The air was thick with coal smoke sifting down from the engines. Each approaching train rumbled past. Astonishingly, Silas grabbed Elliott by the elbow and pushed him upstairs and onto a waiting train. Through a dirty window Elliott could see the mansard roof and ornate façade of the Grand Depot.

A week later Elliott had begun to learn the odd dimensions and curious surfaces of his new life. He was living in a home for newsboys where he could rent a room for a night and store his valuables in his locker—and even get a meal and a shower. He'd learned how to pick up the evening newspapers late in the afternoon and call out the headlines as he walked along. Usually he took twenty papers (Silas was the distributor and staked him to his first armload).

His territory was Wall Street from five to seven, as an army of accountants and brokers rushed home. At first Elliott had been too shy to call out the headlines; he was afraid he didn't sound as if he were from here. But then a fifteen-year-old newsboy from Brooklyn who treated Elliott as if he were a girl and put his cold hand down the back of Elliott's trousers and kissed his neck and breathed the smell of frankfurters and mustard all over him—this redhead Irish boy called Mick, just five foot three, taught him how to bellow out the catchy headlines. "Look, squirt, don't worry if you sounds like some boy soprano—some men like that. A fresh-faced kid like you. Ahh, c'mere, give your old man a hug! That's more like it! Whatcha got back there? Still a virgin? Ooh, look, he's blushin', you's a damn cute little love. Wanna touch my knob? Go ahead, touch it. Want me to prove I'm a real redhead?" Mick guffawed. He sometimes made up fake headlines ("War Declared!" "President Assassinated!") in order to sell his papers in a hurry.

Silas had given Elliott a list of men and addresses who wanted a paper delivered with benefits, that is, "a kiss and a cuddle." They'd paid a dollar for the cuddle, which usually meant the man got down on his knees or expected him to do the work. Elliott didn't mind. Back in his village a hundred years ago he'd stared at the banker and the mayor in their silk cravats, vests buttoned tight over their paunches, trousers held high by wide blue suspenders. He'd been curious about men's flies and good leather shoes and sleeves compressed by silk garters over the biceps. He liked the smells of cigars and witch hazel and of the powder the barber dusted faces and necks with after the daily shave.

Elliott had been afraid of his father—but what he longed for was a younger, handsome, sweet-smelling father-friend who'd take care of him and educate him. He didn't mind his new special customers, unless they failed to be kind. If they just slapped a dollar in his hand and left the room without so much as a fare-thee-well, then he felt bad. When he pleasured himself in his bunk bed late at night at the newsboys' hotel on Rivington Street he moved stealthily so that the bed wouldn't shake. He never thought of any precise deed of darkness but rather of a man stroking his cheek with the back of his hand and offering a whispered word of encouragement.

If the special customers and just the regular passersby didn't purchase all his papers, Elliott would head up to Broadway as the theaters let out. "Last one! Buy my last paper so I can go home and sleep!" he'd call out urgently. And then, after that one was sold, he'd pull out another one from under his coat. "Last one!"

He was proud of his new dishonest ways. He liked accosting a lady in a black fur pelisse and white hat and white silk shirt clinging to a man in white tie and black cutaway and shiny top hat and, in his buttonhole, a huge white flower that had opened in the heat of the theater. Elliott had even learned a popular song, "Please Buy My Last Paper":

> Dark is the night, and the rain it falls fast;
> Sharp is the wind and bitter the blast;
> Yet through rain and darkness there came a lone cry,
> Please buy my last paper, who will buy?

Elliott liked that even his sufferings in New York had been set to a tune; back on the farm he'd been utterly alone with unscored pain.

STEVIE WAS EXHAUSTED. HIS EYES SWAM SHUT AND CORA raised his head so he could enjoy a sip of restorative red wine, though he was half asleep. She was about to leave the room when he said something. She bent closer to hear him.

"Do you like it?"

"Yes, you always surprise me. I didn't know you knew anything about that world."

"Do you?"

"Oh, yes, in my business, you know, we get all types."

"Any suggestions?"

"We used the newsboys to bring new customers our way. Or they'd run errands for the girls, buy them a sandwich or a cooler. Our newsboys in Florida, of course, were little nigger boys."

Stevie smiled. "Should I add that about bringing customers?"

Cora smiled back. She wiped his head with a cool, damp cloth. "Why not? Might as well be hung for a pound if you're hung for a penny—isn't that what they say over here?"

"The whole hog, that's what we say." He smiled, happy to share that hog with her, no matter how figurative.

She'd always found Stevie's style a bit underwritten, but she knew that the best critics liked it that way. Now she wondered if illness hadn't made it *too* spare, even for modern tastes. She doubted that she'd ever be able to sell a fragment (if he didn't live to finish it) of a book about a boy prostitute. *The O'Ruddy* was a much more likely tale of womanizing, tall talk and swordplay. But Stevie enjoyed *The Painted Boy*, she could see that. He'd always been fond of whores—luckily!—and low life was his beat as a journalist. He'd always liked to frequent Chinatown opium dens and Tenderloin fleshpots. Maybe he saw himself in the painted boy as in a distorting mirror.

That night there were no callers. Crane drank a whole bowl of beef bouillon and sat up in bed. He and Cora discussed Conrad.

"He told me once," Cora said, "that he'd learned English reading the Bible. You can be sure he wasn't a believer, but just as surely he always accepted a copy of the Holy Book. They were handed out by the various religious societies for the spiritual welfare of the English sailors on board. Conrad liked the thin Japanese leaves of paper because they were excellent for rolling cigarettes but he always read the page before he smoked it."

Stevie chuckled soundlessly: "I sort of doubt that one. It's a tall tale. He's very systematic about language—he knew French by the time he was five. Though he does have some surprising lapses in English. Today he said he never heard the word *cad*, which I was applying to Oscar Wilde."

"I wish you would stop attacking poor Wilde," Cora said, plumping Stevie's pillows and straightening his blankets. "You, who've become the invert's best friend! It's inconsistent."

They laughed together conspiratorially. Suddenly Cora raised a hand to claim Stevie's attention. "Jessie Conrad told me this afternoon while you and her husband were confabulating in here that when he first saw little baby Borys his comment was as Martian as usual: 'Why it's just like a human being.' Can you believe it? That's what he actually said when he saw his son."

Stevie laughed. He had his big Colt pistol (unloaded) strapped to his side, which he liked to brandish when his European visitors arrived. If he was feeling up to it, he let out a rebel yell and frightened his well-bred friends. Now he drew it out of its holster and pretended to shoot enemies to the right and left.

He started remembering a visit he once paid to Lincoln, Nebraska. He said, "I remember a line of Negro waiters at the Hotel Lincoln. They were serenading the diners. They were accompanied by a storm of strumming banjos. Next door, when I left the hotel, I looked into the office of the *Journal*, where all the electric lights were on cords drawn down from the ceiling and pulled close to the desks. The telegraph sounder was ticking to itself like a bad heart."

"Golly! You always have such a wonderful memory for details. And what a way with words," Cora said, sitting on the bed beside him, stroking his hair.

"That's all I have. It's my stock in trade and my only skill. Not much. But enough." He smiled shyly.

The mention of writing made him ask for a tumbler of whiskey, which Cora poured reluctantly and diluted with a lot of water. Once again he began to dictate.

Elliott met a whore named Imogene. She said she'd pay him a nickel if he'd buy her a cold beer from time to time and bring it to her "establishment," as she called it. She had a radish-white, almost raw-looking body and a tiny head made big by puffed-up hair. He never saw her out of her old torn kimono. She worked at a dollar whorehouse. At the bottom of the mattress, she'd laid a strip of linoleum so that the customers wouldn't have to take their shoes off when they mounted her. They'd just drop their trousers and slide home.

Imogene lived on sunflower seeds and could barely stop munching them, even when she was at work on the bed. She liked Elliott and when he would bring her a customer she'd give him two dimes and call him her "cadet," by which she meant her pimp. Once when she quarreled with her madam she found a room she could rent by the hour from two old sapphists. She asked Elliott to be her full-time cadet and lover. "I could make you some dinner every evening, we'd have a good time together and you'd have some dollars in your pocket." But Elliott told her he wasn't drawn to the sporting life. She just shrugged and ate another handful of sunflower seeds.

What she didn't know was that he'd become a pickpocket. It all happened because Mick, the tough little Irish redhead, was suddenly flush with money he lavished on Elliott. He bought him a sauerbrauten at Luchow's on Fourteenth Street. They ate late in the afternoon toward five o'clock, when they thought few people would "bother them" (look at them). Although it was still light out they sat in the jeweled gloom under the Tiffany-glass ceiling. Elliott was almost afraid to touch the heavily starched white napkin lest he somehow desecrate it. The waiter was a bald German with a stomach and a disapproving frown and a floor-length white apron. The whole place smelled of cabbage and beer. It seemed to Elliott as beautiful as church. They were seated together in a round banquette and Mick drew the tablecloth over their laps and put Elliott's hand directly on his knob, which he'd extricated from his trousers for the occasion. Mick was overexcited because half an hour earlier he'd sniffed cocaine, the pickpocket's drug of choice.

They drank some wheat beer, a pale delicious drink the waiter called "Weissbier." Soon Elliott was ready to fall asleep, and with some difficulty Mick steered him up to a room he'd rented for a day. There on a sagging couch Mick had his way with the frail boy. Elliott liked Mick but wished he were older. A proper man.

Night fell and Elliott could no longer see him, though he could feel his rough fingers on his nipples. Mick said, "Wanna join my mob?"

"Maybe. What is it?"

"It's five friends of mine. We're all engaged in breach-getting."

"Pardon?"

"Throwing the mitt. Pickpocketing. You see, you'd be the stall."

"The—?"

"The guy who asks a fellow a question or stumbles into him or tries to sell him a paper but urgent. And while you've flummoxed him, the dipper (that's me) wires him—that means, picks his pocket."

"Isn't it dangerous?"

"Naw," said Mick, bending in to kiss the boy idly, "specially not if you're a moll-buzzer. If you rob women. If it's a moll we take her book (her pocketbook), and if it's a man we steal his front (his pocketwatch and the chain). We usually make a touch a day."

"Is that how you paid for our dinner?"

"Oh, that was easy, this morning I robbed the Dago in Rome."

"Explain."

"I put a counterfeit five-dollar bill in the collection plate during mass and took back four real ones. Passing fake money we call 'shoving the queer.' "

"Shoving the—?"

Mick pushed him and said suddenly, with a roar of laughter, "That's what I'm doing right now!" Mick then reached down between Elliott's legs, inserted a finger and said, "Mmmn, that feels good!"

Elliott smiled lazily. "If you want me to be a stall you'll have to show me how. But not right now. Right now your knob needs attention again."

Even though he and the mob occasionally made a successful touch by surrounding a man on Fulton or Nassau or lower Broadway or Wall Street, Elliott never stopped selling papers.

One evening Mick convinced him to wear some rather obvious cosmetics—rouge and eyebrow pencil. "You'll see," he said, "a bit of slap will make the men stare and forget themselves, which will help me make the dip. Do the breech-getting."

Elliott suspected Mick himself would derive a perverse

thrill from the paint, but he agreed to the plan with his usual docility. He asked Imogene to help him. She registered his request with a sudden dilation of her pupils: "Oh, I see. *That's* why you didn't want to be my lover."

Elliott neither nodded nor protested. Seconds later she was wetting the tip of her pencil and ordering him to look up. She washed his lips in brandy, then had him bite down on rosy crepe paper. Mick was thrilled with the results: "Oh don't she got a lovely color tonight. The lady Ellen," he said, and grabbed him from behind, nibbled his ear, and whispered, "Wait till I gets you in a dress."

In Union Square, Elliott saw a big awkward man who must've been forty or more but seemed to have recently undergone a spurt of growth since his sleeves scarcely reached down to his sprouting wrists—or maybe his hands were so big and veined they looked as if they'd doubled in size overnight.

Elliott and Mick went up to him with newspapers, thrust them in his face, and then Elliott pretended to stumble and fell into his arms while Mick relieved the man of his gold pocket watch ("banging his red super," in Mick's lingo). Mick ran off but the man held on to Elliott with a look of astonished recognition in his eyes.

"Let me go!" Elliott whined, afraid the man was going to turn him in to the police.

But no, he seemed unaware he'd just been robbed. "I can't let you go," he said hoarsely with a quick sketch of a smile.

He looked at Elliott more closely. "Are you a boy or a girl?"

"A boy."

"I—well, I thought so. That's what . . . interests me."

Elliott was more and more frightened. On the corner he could see Mick waving frantically, then slapping the top of his hand and thrusting it out with a salute. *Run away!* was his meaning. *Take off!*

Elliott relaxed and then suddenly wrenched his body to one side but the man seemed not to register the ruse. He continued to read Elliott's face as if it were an important page in a difficult language.

Elliott changed tactics. "You might as well buy me something to eat in that case."

They were standing in front of the Everett House. The man placed a strong arm behind the boy's back and steered him in past the haughty doorman and, once inside, under the long nose of the outraged manager.

They were seated at a bad table near the kitchen, but the man noticed nothing. He was thunderstruck by something he could detect in Elliott's face—the boy didn't know what it was. Were they relations? Did he see or imagine a resemblance? Did Elliott's red lips, rouged cheeks, and penciled eyes make the man think of some woman he used to love? Or was he a Christian reformer out to save him?

"I must get home soon," the man said, reaching for his pocket watch and then noticing it was gone. "What the hell! What happened—was it that little red-haired devil who picked my pocket?"

"What red-haired devil?" Elliott asked innocently.

"The redhead shortie."

"Oh," Elliott said. "I don't know him. I don't think he's one of the regular newsboys."

"To hell with it," the man said, patting his suit jacket over his heart and reassuring himself that his wallet was still there. "It was a cheap tin watch I bought in Paris when I was a student. *Un oignon*—an onion, that's what the French call it."

A silence sat down at their table like an uninvited guest. At last Elliott said, "I'm sorry someone took your onion."

The man had started reading Elliott's face again as if it were full of bold headlines and long gray paragraphs that detailed all the sorrows of the world and demanded thorough study.

"Why do you look at me like that? Do you think you know me?" He swallowed and said softly, "If so, you're wrong."

The man shook his head as if suddenly pulling free from a bad dream. "No, of course we don't know each other. But we might have in a previous life."

Elliott squirmed in his chair. Outside the dining room window he could see Mick's bright-red hair under a streetlamp as the boy paced rapidly back and forth. Elliott said, "What do you want from me?"

The man looked so dumbstruck that Elliott regretted the question. The man's huge white hands were writhing in his lap. They both stared at the hands as if they were entrails about to be prodded for auguries.

Finally the man hid his hands under the table, sat up, cleared his throat, and said, "Right!" He smiled. "My name is Theodore Koch, I'm a banker, a . . . middling banker, I'm forty-two. I have two children, a boy and a girl, older than you, no doubt. I'd like to spend the rest of my life with you."

Elliott was astounded. Back at the farm he'd often gone to sleep imagining a mayor or banker who'd wait in front of his schoolhouse in a closed carriage, a brougham, the windows heavily curtained, a coachman up above on the box with a long whip in his gloved hand, the whip as slender and electric as a nerve. The mayor or banker would have left the door ajar and, in the dark interior of the brougham, Elliott could just make out the pallor of his face and big white hands, maybe the gleam of a gold watch chain. The boy would approach the carriage and the coachman would jump to the ground to lower three steps and help Elliott up by the elbow. Then he'd retract the stairs, slam the door shut, mount the carriage again, wield his stinging whip, and they'd rush out into the dark, never to return. Startled, Elliott would turn to his savior for his first long look.

"You want to . . . *live* with me?" Elliott asked.

Mr. Koch nodded.

"What about your wife and children?" Elliott asked.

"Oh," Mr. Koch exclaimed, as if he hadn't thought of that objection. His eyes picked over the heavy dull silverware on the table, assessing his options. "Couldn't I just rent a room somewhere for us? In some out-of-the-way, inexpensive neighborhood like Chelsea far from the Fifth Avenue? Too close to the Negro district to be fashionable?"

Elliott frowned, not sure what *fashionable* meant. Nor did he understand Mr. Koch's strange smile. Though the idea of a warm room out of the wet that would be all his own appealed to Elliott, he worried lest Theodore meant to *own* him, or hack him to pieces . . .

"Maybe," Elliott said. "Let's go somewhere now if you have time and *try it on for size*." That was one of the smart things Mick had taught him to say.

Theodore winced at the winking words, then shrugged. "I guess without a watch I have no time, and nothing but time."

They went to a shabby hotel room where Elliott had taken clients before. In bed Elliott was used to something as quick and brutal as rape. But Theodore just held him and stroked him and wept. Theodore had a fleshy, manly body with thighs as big as bolsters and a neat, incongruously small bottom, the least sexual thing Elliott had ever seen, as practical and inoffensive as a little kid's buttocks. He didn't want to turn out the lights, and when Elliott made a dive for his half-hard penis, Theodore drew him back up into his arms. Elliott couldn't see how all this would end. Certainly not in anything as conclusive as spent spunk.

CRANE MUST'VE FALLEN ASLEEP. IN ANY EVENT WHEN HE awakened he wasn't sure how much Cora had written down. Maybe at some point he'd stopped speaking audibly and began simply *thinking* the words, not pronouncing them clearly, or at all. This was a book that was being indicted half on paper and the rest on the tabula rasa of his mind. He'd have to read over everything with care and fill in the blanks.

EIGHT

THAT NIGHT CRANE COULDN'T SLEEP. HE FELT HE'D FALLEN into such a deep slumber while still dictating *The Painted Boy* to Cora that now he wasn't sleepy at all.

He sat up in bed and scooted to the edge and used the chamber pot that was kept handy for him; he wished he could empty it, but just sitting up exhausted him. If he'd had the energy he would have stood and gone to the window and looked down at the boats waiting patiently for the morning crossing to Calais. He could hear the last few carriages clip-clopping past.

He worried how Cora would pay for all this. She swore she had Mr. Frewen's hundred pounds plus three hundred more in cash that she'd squirreled away "in my best Becky Sharpe manner," as she put it. He wanted to believe her but somehow he doubted it; she was just being brave and kind. Of course if he were a decent provider he'd be dictating *The O'Ruddy* and finding someone to finish the manuscript after his death. Robert Barr had refused, but he suggested a young American, Steward Edward White. Barr wrote Cora that Crane's style was too original to imitate: "With pretty near any other man except Kipling and a few others, I would have the cheek to try, but with Stephen, the discrepancy would be too marked." Yes, maybe in *The Red Badge* or "The Open Boat," Crane conceded mentally, but *The O'Ruddy* was pure *Three Musketeers*, only not so good. Easy to copy since it was already an imitation.

His thoughts kept drifting back to Elliott. Maybe because Crane's real brothers—George, Edmund, Townley, Wilbur, and William Howe—were all older, he had always yearned for a disreputable sidekick of a brother, someone who looked up to him and kept getting in trouble. In the Crane family Stevie knew he was loved, but not always admired. *Now* he was, after the success of *The Red Badge* and his coverage of the Spanish-American War, but he knew that for his brothers and sisters he would always be the gifted if suspiciously bohemian little brother, the runt of the litter who didn't lick his paws clean like the other fastidious pups. His hair would always be too shaggy and his face too gaunt. He'd always be outfitted in their eyes with a torn flannel shirt and a slovenly excuse of a necktie, with a greasy fedora and shoes worn down at the heel.

If Stevie could advise Elliott about the ways of the world, Elliott could teach him how to decipher the city around him. Elliott took him to the penny restaurants where the newsboys ate every evening. Food was so important to the boys that they were nicknamed "Pie-Eater" or "Chops" or "Oysters" or "Huckleberry," even "Roundhearts" after a small molasses cake. Elliott liked to munch stale gingerbread cakes called Bolivars and wished the boys would call him "Bolivar." He thought that would be a dashing name. Watermelon was their special treat at a penny a slice. If they were feeling flush (once or twice a year) the boys would sit down to a princely dinner of woodcock and venison.

When they were out walking one evening, Elliott led Stevie

into the one-room windowless apartment where a friend lived with eight brothers and sisters *and* his parents *and* his father's workshop. There the father knocked together wood chairs that the kids would peddle for fifteen cents each.

The room smelled of cooking and body odor and raw wood; two of the children looked rachitic, like shriveled-up little old people with lined faces and missing teeth. They shivered under the threadbare blanket on a sheetless mattress.

Elliott kept himself clean. He spent most nights at a newsboys' home where he rented a bed for six cents, got a free bath and occasionally a haircut for three cents from one of the older boys. Now that Stevie knew him better he realized that there was something cool and elegant about Elliott, as if he were the Lost Dauphin. He seemed to have gone directly from extreme timidity to a faintly arrogant standoffishness, a quick relabeling of many of the same characteristics.

Elliott loved the populous city, with its miles and miles of slums, those mephitic tenements spread out everywhere and quick with noise and drunken brawls, banging doors and rank cooking smells, unlit passageways and rickety stairs, the sense that every wall and door was just the thinnest possible membrane holding back a boiling larval mess soon to explode and metamorphose into more and more sticky life.

Together they followed fire wagons and black mariahs, visited bordellos and chatted up the girls. Like all the newsboys Elliott loved the low theater. He dragged Stevie along to the vaudeville acts he preferred to see with strongmen and boxers, female impersonators, dancing bears, banjo players, and "The Devil's Cave," an exciting new fire act. They saw *Dick Turpin*, a play about a famous thief that included the execution of the hero right on stage. At the Bowery Theatre they saw a ballet of scantily clad women; on the sidewalk afterwards Elliott tried to dance on his toes till Crane made him stop.

All of the rush and boom and slither on the stage was more than matched by the noisy audience's wisecracks. Stephen especially liked the signs that told the audience not to snack, drink, smoke, boo too loudly, or rush the aisles, though not one of these injunctions was obeyed. In fact, the signs only served to remind everyone to practice these very noxious habits.

Stephen asked Elliott more than once if he'd ever thought of combining pickpocketing with selling newspapers but Elliott looked scandalized, then smiled his shy geisha smile with his hand over his bad teeth and confessed, "I'd be afraid." Even so, in *The Painted Boy* Stephen would attribute petty theft to Elliott, since he had already researched it and learned the lingo from an ex-con for a *Herald* article he wanted to write. Anyway, theft had provided a dramatic way to introduce Elliott to Theodore Koch, the married man. Crane didn't know how they'd actually met (Elliott never told him), but Crane could never forget the face of that man waiting on the street for them outside the Slide.

Stephen remembered the afternoon when he'd met Jennie. Elliott, with an air of a curator bringing out the prized piece in his collection, took him to an apartment near the Fifth Avenue and the Central Park Zoo. It was in a new building in a Beaux Arts style— the sort of residence, Stephen thought, I would never have imagined belonging to one of Elliott's friends. We went up four flights to the top floor where someone had left the front door ajar.

Elliott told me on the way that Junie was the one who'd been his "queer mother." She (or he?) had taught him how to be queer, and when Elliott was cold and hungry and hadn't sold his papers he could always sleep on Jennie's couch. "She's just a friend. A mother. Of course we'd never do anything . . . of that sort. She just likes me. She takes care of me."

Inside, drapes had been drawn over closed curtains to create a crepuscular atmosphere. A suffocating odor of tuberose, too aggressive to be accommodated and forgotten, clung to heavy store-bought family furniture that had been sprinkled with lace throws and antimacassars as dainty as ocean foam. A grandfather clock ticked like a time bomb.

At last the occupant of the apartment appeared, brushing through a portiere of fringe dangling over the bedroom door. He seemed to be a man—at least his hands were large and his Adam's apple prominent—but he shuffled along with a slave girl's traipsing gait, and indeed he had bangles around his ankles just below his silk harem pants. Something floating and diaphanous sheathed his thick torso; through the layers of sheer fabric one could see large female breasts.

"Hello," a dark contralto voice said, "I'm Jennie June, sometimes known as Ralph, or Earl."

Elliott and I had no such multiple identities to disclose, so the introductions were quickly made.

Jennie led us back to two armchairs and, for herself, an uncomfortable-looking side chair with a gilded bamboo back. Her hips appeared very wide and she settled down on the flimsy cane bottom like a matronly bird on a very small nest. "It's fortunate for me," Jennie said coolly, "that you're not one of my many types. If you were bigger or rowdier or more athletic I'd be trying to seduce you the whole time."

"I *am* athletic," I said, instantly regretting the flare-up of my pride that made me sound as if I wanted to be eligible for this creature's attentions. I gulped, "Or rather I *was*."

"Ah, we all have a glorious past. I, for instance, *was* a man, but two years ago I was castrated at my request. The intention of such a drastic intervention was to ablate my libidinous desires, which had gotten out of hand. Between the ages of twenty and thirty-two I had enjoyed the favors of nearly three thousand men and had developed a passion for practicing *fellatio*, placing their *membra virilia in ore*." My Latin was fairly impressionistic but I was certain a cock in the mouth was being discussed.

"Sometimes it is my delight to place the *membra intra femora meius*." *Between the thighs? He likes to be browned between his locked thighs?*

Jennie June crooned, "As you can see, I am a highly respectable person of an upper-middle-class background. And I am of a scholarly turn of mind and, when I know you better, I'll divulge to you more about my academic pursuits."

That was rich—he was more modest about his studies than his sex life. His face, glabrous and plucked clean of eyebrows, he turned toward me as if presenting me with a wide dish of blanc-mange. "How do you fit in," I asked, "your academic life with your hobby as a bisexual?" I'd picked up that he liked the word *bisexual* to refer to a man-woman who slept with men.

"*Hobby!*" He shrieked with indignation. "You're an outrage!" Like a mother hen he rose partly from his nest, ruffled his feathers and then sat magnificently back down. "Well you might ask," he said in a more conciliatory tone, "if I'd given myself free rein, I would've never amounted to anything. Luckily, I had self-discipline to confine my *sprees* (for that is what I called them) to one day every fortnight. But, heavens! I'm forgetting my hostessly duties. Would you like a very special tea with bits of dried orange and bergamot in it?"

"With pleasure," I said. Elliott was hypnotized by our host's grand manner and appeared to be memorizing his "upper-middle-class" ways and my elegant replies.

When we'd settled down again I said to this ageless, sexless creature, "As a mere man I can't imagine having as many conquests as you've accumulated."

"Well, my dear," he said, sipping delicately without slurping, and looking up with round eyes over the rim of the cup, "I've always had a *faiblesse* for our young warriors, those earthly embodiments of the great god Mars. I discovered a military camp not far from here, in White Plains to be exact—biscuit?" And he offered me a pink ladyfinger, before taking one himself and inspecting it from all sides, then consuming it in two bites. He continued to speak with the mouthful of pink biscuit clearly visible, like a thicker, younger, tongue, one that had somehow come loose. Maybe he thought as a lady he should feast only on pink foods, for he also downed several heavily iced pink cupcakes.

He suddenly clapped his hands together like a child. "Oh, I love soldiers! I met one at the entrance to the camp and told him I admired his muscles and sun-bronzed neck and his wide chest and deep voice. I said that I might easily swoon—and I did in reality half-stumble—in the presence of such martial virility! He blushed like a boy and in a choked-up voice asked me my name. 'Jennie June,' I said brightly and he asked me, with a dawning smile, if I were a boy in girl's clothes. I put my hands over my ears and wagged my head furiously side to side: 'Not so many dreadful questions!' I added, gurgling in baby talk, 'I'm neither fish nor fowl, I'm a iddle-widdle baby, just a tiny whiney babykins,' and he laughed gaily and said, 'Maybe the baby needs a bottle? Something to suck on? Such a hungry little baby.' And I was charmed by how fast he was, for I've always insisted intelligence is a matter of quickly resetting one's dials and who could be faster than Corporal Courtney?"

I nodded vaguely, not sure what I was committing myself to and certain the corporal must have been desperately randy if he'd fallen under the spell of this thick-thighed zephyr.

"I soon became the daughter of the regiment," Jennie June said complacently, fanning herself with a letter, not because it was hot but for rhetorical effect. "I would just show up to the entrance of the barracks wearing mascara and a semitransparent blouse but baggy men's trousers that nonetheless revealed my ample hips." He stood suddenly and turned slowly around to show me their amplitude. "One of my colleagues at work recently paid me the compliment of saying, 'Ralph, you are a tub of mush! You look like a fat *Frau* in the last stage of pregnancy!'"

I wasn't quite sure why Ralph should like this description except that it did fully acknowledge his femininity. I smiled weakly.

"At the barracks some of the soldiers treated me roughly and even shoved me, saying I was an abomination, but the corporal was kind, and besides, there was a fire of lust burning in his eyes, so he protected me. I said, 'They want to spank the iddle-widdle baby but baby hasn't been naughty, no, no!'"

"And did he keep you all to himself?" Pulling out my reporter's notepad. "Is it all right?" I asked, nodding toward my pen.

"I'm relieved you're taking notes," Jennie/Ralph said with a sagacious nod. The implication was that he knew that he was a natural subject for journalistic investigation and he preferred open professional curiosity to veiled slipshod amateurism. "No," Jennie said, "he shared me with his friends. As long as they were willing to rock me in their arms and call me their darling baby, I was happy to perform *fellatio* on them."

He pronounced it "fell-ah-tee-oh," in the Latin fashion. He

obviously saw himself as an object of scientific inquiry *and* an avatar of the Classical tradition.

"But which are you in your heart of hearts?" I asked. "A girl or a baby?"

"Well you might ask. I was happiest when I performed as the French Doll Baby in a cabaret on the Bowery. We dolls wear gowns of an art design—Art Nouveau—and we're little 'fraidy-cat babies who weep easily, but we can be gay and sing along like pert misses, so *fly*, playing to a stalwart guy. Here's a poem I translated from the French:

> *'Little tootsy-wootsy!' cries Guy,*
> *'Art ravishingly cute!*
> *Thou art, yea, a pretty Pussie! Pussie! Pussie!*
> *Ne'er saw I such a beaut.' "*

As I sat there watching this deformity-pudding rave on about her youth I became more and more depressed. All too easily I could imagine the scorn or even murderous rage she must have awakened in her day and indeed soon she was talking about Harvey, a jailbird whom she offered to keep since he was so strong, such a hero, a titan, a Hercules. Until Harvey led her into a dark alley in the wasteland of gas-houses, closed factories, and storeyards beside the East River, robbed her, and beat her so badly she couldn't leave her apartment for two weeks afterwards. I wondered if Elliott would, over the years, become more and more like her. But Elliott would never have this comfortable apartment to retreat to. And Elliott would have no safe, middle-class life as an alternative.

Jennie recounted more horrors she'd endured at Harvey's hands. And yet all she could say now, years later, was that if she ever saw Harvey again, her hero-boy, she'd walk up behind him and whisper, "Supreme Man."

"I'm sure," she said, "that he'd recognize me, for certainly no one else in his crowd of rowdies and illiterates has ever called him Supreme Man. The naughty, foolish man, he rejected my magnanimous offer to send him to university so that he might win a respectable position in society as a doctor or a lawyer—rejected me just for the fleeting pleasure of striking me down in an ignominious alleyway, and only because he had been taught by society that an androgyne is Satan's child."

He told us how he'd often trip up and down the Rialto, by which he meant Fourteenth Street between Broadway and Second Avenue, in full makeup and with his gurgling baby-like cooing and a mincing walk, and how on that short strip he'd meet and greet the cardsharps and fancy ladies, the small-time crooks and sister androgynes or "female-impersonators," as he sometimes called them. If she saw a man she liked she'd try to lure him up Second Avenue to Stuyvesant Square, an outdoor park that was looked down upon by the chaste façade of the Quaker church.

"Or laughing and gurgling like a delighted baby girl, I might lead him to Paresis Hall on the Bowery at Fifth Street. The habitués never called it 'Paresis,' which after all is the final stage of madness in syphilis—they called it simply 'the Hall.' In fair weather it had a beer garden out back. I can well remember seating myself there, while at adjoining tables rang out the shrieks and guffaws of the androgynes, young bloods and 'soubrettes,' by which I mean genital females. I quickly learned that my sister androgynes had assumed names such as 'Manon Lescaut' and 'Prince Pansy,' though Manon's only sign of her femininesqueness was her wide hips. Another androgyne (who curiously enough used a male sobriquet, Roland Reeves) looked feminine only because of his natural beardlessness and pink-peony cheeks. He, Roland, approached my table and invited me to join his club, the Cercle Hermaphroditos. He said, 'We care to admit only extreme types, true glandular cases who like to doll themselves up. We must stand united against the world's persecution of bisexuals. After all, our only fault is that in one out of one hundred and fifty presumed males the internal testicular secretion has failed to be of the right consistency.' "

"And yet," I objected, though I knew that my objection would raise a storm of pedantic Latinate argument, "your drive could only be that of a man. Only a man could have such a voracious appetite."

"Have you never heard of Messalina? Of Catherine the Great? Oh, my dear, history is full of splendid, reckless nymphomaniacs."

I just shrugged and said, "Overruled."

As Jennie prattled on, I noticed that her speech was peppered with such falsely elegant, freshly minted expressions as "beardal hair" for *beard*, "glabricity" for *hairlessness*, the "Noachian deluge" for the *flood*, and "I experience only detestation" for *I detest*. She made me smile.

He offered to accompany us to a masked ball. Apparently he had a "hypermasculine" escort, a certain Tony Neddo, to accompany him. "You will be impressed by Tony's heroic masculinism, though he has only the meager education of the rural districts of Ireland."

The plan for her was to go to Paresis Hall in men's clothes and there change into full female finery. Jennie had already bought a knee-length turquoise satin gown in which she would interpret Euterpe. She'd sewn gold-dipped sleigh bells to lace flounces on the shoulders and sleeves. "Whenever I will move, they will emit a melodious jingle," she said, lowering her eyes modestly. "And then I'll be wearing openwork stockings of an azure hue and pumps of purple kid with mother-of-pearl buckles. My chevelure will be surmounted by a gold-plated lyre, studded with hundreds of Paris diamonds. And I promise you you'll be surrounded by wonderful creatures—monkeys, geese, foxy grandpas, Happy Hooligans, Mephistopheles . . ."

Although I am as susceptible to female beauty as the next man, women's talk of clothes has always bored me witless.

I kept looking at Elliott and wondering if in a few years he'd be parroting all this absurd twaddle. Obviously Jennie and "the ladies" we'd met at the Slide had no idea of what made them tick. Jennie, with his breasts and wide hips, did seem the victim of a physical imbalance, and his appetites did appear to be driven and dangerously out-of-whack, despite his volitional castration. But I couldn't see anything strange about Elliott's looks or body. He was the usual skinny-hipped, flat-stomached, tightly wound, narrow-chested, knobby-shouldered teenage boy even if he did put on ladylike airs, awkwardly, in a dumb boyish way. His feet and hands were too large for his frame; he had the exhausted look of someone still growing, when he didn't look surprised at his very existence. I suspect that back on the farm he'd been a frightened drudge who lived intensely off his daydreams (of escape, of salvation). Now he was inhabiting an intersexual world of such fantastic dimensions that he no longer needed to daydream. Perhaps he feared that sometime soon he'd wake up and he'd be back in that bleak, unheated house outside Utica with his lanky, belligerent brothers and sadistic father.

Jennie June's newest rant crowded out my thoughts: "My precious *convives*, don't you just know your little baby Jennie has to be oh-so-careful when I'm all dolled up because on three separate occasions I've been pursued by Stuyvesant Square clubmen—that's what I call the ruffians who prey on us hermaphrodites and fairies. Usually I slip away unnoticed and board the elevated train all unseen, but three times I've been dogged by clubmen, determined to force their way into my apartment to rob me. Fortunately all three times I detected them before heading home. When I descended from the El I just sat down on the first bench and outwaited them, though twice I so outraged them that they punched me in the face."

As Jennie went on describing her travails, Elliott's eyes got bigger and bigger, as if he could see the thugs and feel the blows.

We left Jennie after many decorous farewells, made slightly disconcerting because she had pink cupcake frosting smeared on her face just below her left cheek—for in her greed she had missed her mouth.

When we came downstairs onto the street, there on the opposite curb stood the married man, Theodore Koch, waiting for us. He looked like Watteau's Gilles, the overgrown clown with the grown-up, unfunny face and the awkward body of a harlequin; in the painting Gilles has somehow been hoisted up on the stage and below him, as if in the orchestra pit, are laughing faces wearing commedia dell'arte masks. Now there were no faces nor masks, but the sound of mocking laughter was subsumed in Koch's ashamed features.

"Wait here," Elliott said.

He went across the street and spoke to Theodore. I couldn't hear what Elliott was saying but I could see that he was trying to pacify the man by making quieting gestures. Theodore looked crestfallen. If he was jealous the whole situation struck me as ridiculous and I was tempted to cross the street and introduce myself . . .

NINE

ORA TOLD STEPHEN THE NEXT MORNING THAT SHE THOUGHT he was strong enough to make the voyage across the Channel. There'd been a mix-up about renewing their American passports. In normal circumstances they would have had to go to the American Embassy in London, but due to the "special circumstances," the consular agent in Dover had been officially instructed to come to the hotel to take their sworn statements; he was supposed to issue them the documents later today.

Just to make chitchat (and because the matter directly concerned him), Cora recounted all the copious details of the passport affair, all the he-said she-said particulars, but at last Stevie held up a hand, as if to ward off the hailstorm of words. He said, "I *can't* . . ." She stopped, not disconcerted or angry, but awed by his upraised hand. He'd always been game for "real life," as they jokingly called it, the sordid details about the drunk cook who had to be replaced and the snobbish coachman who quit without notice, all the funny things Mrs. Conrad said about Henry James's fear that some of his august friends might accidentally meet the

Cranes, who weren't properly married, whose lives were "irregular"—oh, Stevie had always been game for the net full of gossip Cora spread out at his feet at least once a day, for if he was an imaginative writer, one who could invent people and incidents *ex nihilo*, she was a mimetic artist in both her conversation and her writing. She brought him all these ugly scraps hoping he'd sew them into a beautiful quilt. Now, however, with those words *I can't*, and his raised protective hand, Stevie revealed he couldn't cope with the world anymore, with "real life," and she saw that his renunciation was irrevocable.

From now on all his energies would be consecrated to survival—to the trip to the Black Forest. And to this strange little book, *The Painted Boy*.

She wondered if the "affair" between Theodore and Elliott was Stevie's adult, dying self revisiting the vital kid he'd once been. She *esteemed* Stevie too highly—as a free spirit, a devoted lover, a shining artist, a stainless journalist—to question this latest and possibly last endeavor. But she couldn't help probing it, gently, as one would look at a wound.

Was he expressing feelings he always harbored but never dared let out? But no, that was impossible. She understood men, how some looked at other men with rivalry, others with hate and some with friendly competition, still others with indifference—and the few with desire. But Stevie didn't desire other men; he liked most people with a canine friendliness and an acquired amused skepticism. Ten men and boys could troop past him stark naked and he wouldn't even look up from his book except to tease one about his bottom turned red from sitting too long.

At the first rustle of a bombazine skirt, however, his eyes would swivel like a bird-dog's pointing a pheasant. And he noticed things, like the size of a woman's breasts, of course, but also the turn of her slender ankle and the softness of her hand, the soaring beauty of her neck supporting a head too large to be lovely. And women's caprices and needs he could anticipate, the moment when they wanted to leave the party, or undo their stays.

And now, when she thought of that gesture he'd made, warding her off or at least her words, her demands, it occurred to her that Stevie might be vexed by the way she'd taken charge, though she had no choice. She was the one who had to orchestrate every detail of this elaborate trip to France and thence to Bavaria. She was the one who had to raise the money, line up the nurses, secure the rooms here and there. And she was the one who had to dun their agent, their rich friends and publishers here and in the States.

Maybe Stevie resented her usurpation of his powers, though on the other hand he always used her as a secretary. But maybe now—she couldn't quite grasp her own idea—maybe now he was asserting his independence from her by inventing a story that had nothing to do with her. An all-male world that excluded her.

He said, "I'd like to sit up and dictate some more. I promise I'll get back to *The O'Ruddy*, but for now—"

"Shhh," she said, smiling. "Dearest. You're the boss. Or, in this case, the dictator."

He laughed. She thought her hunch might be accurate. He was turning her into the witness of an all-male world, of men loving men, and that wasn't a great rupture in their lives but merely a minor way of rebuking her gentle tyranny.

THE PAINTED BOY (*continued*)

Theodore got winded climbing the four flights he'd rented for Elliott. The days were growing darker earlier, and colder, and though it was only four-thirty Theodore hoped the day-light would hold since there were no lamps in their room yet. He wanted Elliott to receive a good impression of the room. All that was in it so far, as best he could remember, was a single bed and a chair and a chifforobe. Down the hall was a tiny toilet and, behind the door, on the other side, a sink. Theodore had just bought a pitcher and bowl for washing up in the room.

Theodore felt the key in his pocket for the third time. Its jagged teeth on one side and smooth back on the other felt like a scaled-down containable version of everything he'd hoped for. He looked back at Elliott, who was just a few steps below him. He'd wanted the boy to go first so Elliott wouldn't observe him struggling up four flights. But Elliott kept ushering the man forward with a funny gesture of his right hand, almost as if he were scattering seed.

There were dubious sounds and smells in the stairwell, though at this hour surely most of the residents must be at work. Maybe their wives were already preparing supper.

Theodore imagined his wife thought he was having an affair with another woman. He guessed that from little things she said and did. Just last Sunday she'd insisted that they should go to church after months of not attending, as if a reminder of the sacraments would make him straighten out. While kneeling he thought of Elliott. Elliott's naked body.

Theodore, who admitted he was too portly, now reached their landing. He was seeing stars and breathing heavily. He looked back at Elliott, who was still two steps behind and below him, wearing the newsboy's cap that writer fellow had bought him. It wasn't that Theodore pictured doing lascivious things to Elliott, at least not usually; that wasn't why he stripped him mentally when he thought about him. Elliott did not look like himself when he was dressed, just as Napoleon was said not to have resembled himself if seen from the left side rather than the right side, or head-on. In clothes, Elliott looked cramped, old-mannish, his face as white as winter; but once he cast them aside he recovered his summery boyishness.

"No, wait," Theodore said, holding out a hand. He inserted the key, pushed the door open, lifted Elliott in his arms and carried him over the threshold. Elliott weighed dangerously little.

The boy looked around the room a bit listlessly and without much comprehension, like a Red Indian contemplating his first Rubens. Maybe in his backward, motherless family the boys had never learned to show enthusiasm or even curiosity, much less gratitude. Or maybe he was unimpressed; perhaps he had many rich clients who invited him back to sumptuous quarters. Or maybe in fact he was overwhelmed and unable to show it, deprived of the simplest language of acknowledgment. Or maybe, like Theodore's own son, Robin, he was determined not to gratify Theodore by expressing the expected emotion. Or maybe—

Oh, it was hopeless, trying to guess what Elliott was thinking. The boy was naturally reticent, and the less he said the more Theodore heard himself stuttering, sighing, finishing unspoken sentences for him.

"Well?" Theodore asked. He shrugged his bulky body out of the heavy overcoat and threw his garment on the bed. He'd left the ewer and bowl on the floor outside. Now he brought them in and closed the door. To fill the silence Theodore removed the packaging and centered the new objects on the hardwood floor near the window.

"Is it really mine?" Elliott asked tonelessly. The boy was looking out the window and the last glow in the sky disclosed the ratty little garden below, just a few leafless brambles in the mud.

Theodore was standing beside him and put his arm around the boy's slender waist. "Here's the key, the one and only key. It's all yours." He paused. "Not much, but it's home, eh?"

Elliott turned toward him and kissed him on the cheek. Theodore worried that someone across the way might see them.

"Undress me," Elliott whispered. "If we're lying down, we're so high up no one will be able to see in."

"The bank . . ." Theodore feebly protested. He was due back, though the estimable Mr. Stallman, his assistant, would cover for him once again, no doubt.

No, it was something else; when Theodore wasn't with Elliott all he could do was think about the boy. When he was with him, however, he was so anxious he couldn't wait to leave, as if he needed solitude to recreate the boy's image in his mind, to worship it at the correct distance.

For years—for a decade!—many things, most things, in Theodore's life had been predictable and stable and had grown stale. Of course there was little Robin's terrible bout of mumps, the impossibly high fevers that only ice packs and cold drinks and venesection with leeches had been able to bring down—the poor little tyke had been drained of seventy ounces of blood altogether.

And then there was the birth of little Josephine, who was

delivered with much more pain than Robin, and only after ten hours of excruciating labor.

After Josephine's birth Theodore's wife, Christine, had never wanted to make love again. Perhaps she now associated intimacy with pain. Or maybe her maternal joys and sorrows replaced her womanly desires; he'd heard of such cases. Josephine had been frail and underweight at birth; Christine had moved her next to her bedroom and usually kept the door open so that she might hear the slightest stirring or cry.

For the next decade Theodore had kept to his own little room. He'd gratified himself at the table with second helpings of buttery dishes and rich desserts. At lunchtime he consumed three courses at his club around the corner from the bank. His tailor had let out his suits without comment beyond saying quietly, "We can always let them out a bit more next year if you like—just bring them in." No one commented on his "bay window" except for Mr. Niedermayer, the bank president, who found such "added adipose" gratifying in a man since he himself overindulged and liked to refer to his "Jovian girth," as if it truly were godlike. Niedermayer's stomach did not really go with his spindly long arms and legs.

Now Theodore sat at one end of the single bed, out of eyeshot, and had Elliott stand facing him. He slowly undressed him, starting with his little cap and jacket and working his way down, bending over to unlace the shoes, pulling them off, one by one, as the boy steadied himself on the man's shoulders. Then the stockings, then the trousers and undergarments.

A sharp smell of crabgrass and sperm, sweet, almost lactic, lifted off the newly liberated body, for it had been freed from every sign that it belonged to this century rather than to some remote bucolic one. Now he stood in front of him like a portable deity, the presence, at once domestic and sacred, unveiled to protect the hearth. Theodore remembered that when he was a boy, Catholic neighbors had invited the priest in to bless their just completed house. That's what Theodore was doing, except that he was exposing the sacred heart of his little love to consecrate this shabby room.

Theodore suddenly had a brilliant idea. "You should pose for a sculptor, Elliott. If I had a statue of you, a nude statue, I could live with it night and day. After all, a banker of my importance"—and here Theodore smiled at his own absurdity—"should own neoclassical works and display them in his drawing room, don't you think?"

Elliott smiled at him vaguely and shook his head in disbelief.

"What?" Theodore asked.

Elliott said, "You'd sit in your living room with your wife and children and a nude statue of me?"

"Of course—a thing of beauty is a joy forever."

Elliott put his hands behind his head, revealing the corn silk floating in his armpits. "Besides," Elliott said with a little smile, "it would never work. Those guys in sculptures have small knobs. I've seen statues. And mine, as you know at firsthand, is all too large."

Theodore smiled, though he really didn't like it when Elliott was bawdy.

The next day Theodore bought a curtain on a rod and a

hammer and nails. He stood on the chair and banged it into place.

"So no daylight for me, then?"

"You can use some string to tie the sides together during the daylight hours. I'll bring you a lamp tomorrow."

Day after day Theodore added one little thing after another—a washcloth, dried biscuits, a second pillow, a clean set of sheets, a book about *Ragged Dick the Newsboy* by Horatio Alger, subtitled *Street Life in New York*. It was supposed to be edifying.

Theodore always came at five now; he lied and told his wife he was studying Italian with an elderly gentleman from Florence because he wanted to have the best accent when they made their grand voyage to the Continent in another year.

It wasn't that Theodore hoped to be rid of Christine, or to live with Elliott. He didn't think ahead, though usually it was in the nature of love to plan. Rather, he wanted everything to continue exactly as it was—his position at the bank, his hour a day with Elliott's warm naked body seated on his lap, the substantial meals at home on Sixteenth Street, his goodnight kisses with his children, the half-hour alone in bed before he fell asleep during which he could think about Elliott's tiny, sensitive ears he nibbled while he stood behind him, the deep, bluish shadow hollowed out above his prominent clavicles, the high instep of feet that were marred by a farmer's horny nails, the way his face looked at once so young and so weary. Weary because of the dark circles under his eyes and the down-sweep of his mouth. Young because his nose and ears were still diminutive with youth, and the wings of his nose were oily and rough with nearly invisible bumps that could someday flare up into acne spots but probably would not. Young because an artist could have drawn each contour of his features with a single flowing line, none yet irregular or quirky with age. Young because his sealskin eyebrows formed a lovely, rounded legato mark. Young because his hair was shiny, his cheek beardless, his pores chamois-small (except on the nose, where they were inflamed around the nostrils), his breath slightly decayed, his teeth as whittled by caries as dominos by black dots. Young because his lower lip was always moist, a patch of brightness a painter might have rendered with a single charged dab of titanium white.

If there were fairies (or androgynes) on the one hand and men on the other, real men, then Theodore didn't know which roles to assign to them. Obviously Theodore was the man, but he didn't like the idea of Elliott being a female stand-in. His boyishness, which sometimes seemed as antique as Attic Greece itself, was what he prized, though admittedly he had first been attracted to (galvanized by) the ambiguity of his painted face. Was that because the mascara revealed how desperate the boy was, how extreme, and, therefore, how available? The paint showed that he was an object of desire, someone for sale, which boys never were.

Theodore was amused by Elliott's affectations, partly because he carried them off so badly. But even if inexpert, his posing demonstrated the differences between them. Elliott was small and smooth and elastic. He was so slender that he did seem to be a different creature altogether, only not feminine, and he was always trying out a new style of behavior, though it never actually fit him.

"Are you ever attracted to your own son?" Elliott asked

one afternoon. "He's about my age, isn't he? Is he handsome?"

"Never," Theodore said. "The thought has never crossed my mind. I love my son with a melancholy, impatient love, partly because I see so much of myself in him. He's a plodder like me, doesn't usually get the joke, is nervous for no reason and, like me, taps his foot all the time. He has a nice way with people, a sort of blinking, startled, completely uncalculating niceness. I suppose he's good-looking, though he's not athletic, and he has an overbite and already wears glasses, which are always smudged with thumbprints. I like him on the days when I like myself."

Out of the blue Elliott asked, "Do I make you like yourself?"

And just as quickly Theodore said, "On the days when *you* like me, I like myself immoderately."

One day Elliott asked, "What are you going to do when you get to Italy and you can't speak Italian of any sort, much less with the right accent?"

"Oh, but I do speak a bit of Italian already." Theodore thought it over and said, "Once in a while I start to imagine all the disasters that lie in wait for me, and then I can't sleep. But most of the time I push it all out of my mind."

"Like what? What sort of disasters?"

"That you'll leave me for someone richer or more amusing. That my wife will see us together. That I'll lose my job. That I'll end up in the gutter. That we'll dock in Genoa and I won't remember the word for baggage."

"What is it?"

"Bagagli."

Elliott practiced saying it just by moving his lips, not

making a sound. At last he said, "No one is as good and kind as you. Why would I leave you? As for *amusing*, that means nothing to me . . . a lot of the other newsboys are funny enough."

Theodore had no idea how Elliott passed his days. He knew that Elliott still sold papers, though no longer during the full evening shift since he invariably spent from five to six with Theodore. He took the leftover copies a frail little friend of his hadn't managed to unload during rush hour and peddled them late at night at the entrances to theaters or at elevated trains or in front of restaurants. Theodore once caught sight of him when he came out of Delmonico's with Mr. Niedermayer.

Elliott bought his Bolivars and frankfurters with the pennies he'd earned. Theodore was tempted to give him an allowance but he didn't want to rob the boy of ambition. Ragged Dick, after all, worked hard and saved money and rose in the world. He hoped that Elliott might find a trade or occupation that would catch his fancy.

If Theodore gave free rein to his imagination, it pulled him over the cliff like one of Plato's passionate horses. He could become so jealous that soon he wasn't concentrating on his work and could barely bring himself to authorize the piles of checks that Mr. Stallman placed before him for his signature every afternoon at three. Through the smoked-glass screening of his office he could see shadowy figures passing like the vague images that tormented him. Elliott lying in his bed with another man. Elliott taking a paper up to a "special customer," who grabbed him and pulled him in for five minutes in the pantry. Elliott at the Slide or Paresis Hall with those sickening "female impersonators" and their soul-killing "advice." Elliott with that fiendish, red-haired accomplice who stole his pocket watch, his *oignon* . . .

For Elliott in his laconic way had confided just scraps enough to inflame Theodore's jealous mind. Elliott had somehow recovered the stolen *oignon* and returned it to Theodore, but refused to say how he'd managed that. When they first met, Elliott had smilingly described his "newsboy prostitute ring" and had even offered to procure another kid for them. Theodore had indignantly refused ("I don't like *boys*, I love *you*") and later had grilled him at such length—demanding names and descriptions—that Elliott had refused to disburse any more information. Usually Theodore was a tranquil man, a daydreamer, but now he was alert and agitated.

And then Theodore had seen Elliott talking to that shaggy small writer or journalist, Stephen Crane, who Elliott claimed liked women exclusively and was "interviewing" Elliott just to get his story.

"Have you told him about us?" Theodore demanded. "Of course you have, but for God's sake don't give him my name." To himself, Theodore thought, you have nothing to lose, Elliott, but I have everything. "And how do I know you don't sleep with Crane?"

"Does Mr. Crane look boy-simple to you?" Elliott demanded, indignant.

"Boy-what?"

"Wild about boys: boy-simple."

"No, he doesn't, but do I?" And here Theodore drew the naked Elliott to his lap. "And yet I am. I'm simple about you."

Theodore nudged him slightly forward so he could kiss the falling drops of vertebrae that descended from his nape to his coccyx. Theodore liked the boy to be naked but he preferred to remain in his own undergarments. He was tormented by every concrete detail of Elliott's body. The long fingers that didn't taper but passed evenly from joint to joint like bamboo. The faintly disagreeable acrid smell of the water closet after Elliott used it. The way his arms were almost as slender at the shoulder as they were at the wrist.

"Does he give you presents?"

"Mr. Crane? Only my cap. He has no money. And why should he give me things? He doesn't want anything from me." And here Elliott smiled. "Not like a certain big poppa bear I know who wants to put his finger in the honey pot."

Everything Elliott said tormented him with shame and jealousy and desire. He was ashamed of his desires and yet he couldn't tame them. Just hearing the words *honey pot* caused a stirring throughout his body. There was something jarring and depressing and weirdly thrilling about hearing his desire referred to in such vulgar and readymade terms.

Each day Elliott was picking up more slang and the funny, semi-theatrical gestures of the duchesses at the Slide. If Theodore would thank him for something, Elliott might hold out the hem of his jacket and bob a curtsy. If he was trying to persuade Theodore to provide him with relief, he'd say, "Why don't you kiss the worm?" Once he said, "Does your son Robin wear a low neck and short sleeves?" When Theodore looked blank, Elliott said, "Is he *circumcised*, dummy?"

Theodore was horrified by the idea that there was a whole culture of perversion, if you could call it that. He wanted them to be Robinson Crusoe and Friday on a queer island of their own devising, every moment of their life something they'd invented.

And yet, in spite of himself, he wanted, out of jealousy no doubt, to know more and more about this funhouse world that Elliott was being inducted into. At the Slide, to perform fellatio was "to blow the skin flute," whereas the same act man-to-woman became "to sneeze in the cabbage." Of a man who imagined no one suspected he was homosexual, though everyone might know, it was said that he was "wearing a cut-glass veil." A "bronco" was a boy who was just being broken into homosexuality.

One day Elliott, pulling Theodore by the tie into a deep kiss, said, "You're a jam"—and then explained, "a jam, just a man."

If a sissy man and a real woman made love, the duchesses said dismissively, "Another sister-act." If a fairy turned to women and a normal life, it was said that he had "lost his gender." Mutual masturbation was "chopsticks."

"I guess you know," Elliott said once, "that I'm called a prick-peddler. A prostitute."

"Wouldn't you like to learn a proper trade?" Theodore asked earnestly but with not much enthusiasm for a future he could not actually believe in. He wanted to cast a spell that would freeze them in the positions they already occupied, to be freed only a hundred years hence by a princely and charming kiss. He could not imagine any good coming out of any change whatsoever. "Perhaps in the twenty-first century," he said.

"I don't know," Elliott said, yawning, "Perhaps," he added vaguely. He, too, seemed incapable of imagining the future, or of learning a trade.

When they made love, Theodore was moved to see the look of concentration and curiosity that caused Elliott to squint and even half-smile as he looked down at what was being done to him; he whispered once, "That's what I really like . . ."

Several times Theodore caught Elliott in the company of Stephen Crane—most recently coming out of an elegant Art Nouveau apartment building in the East Sixties. "Caught" wasn't the right word, since Theodore had shadowed them assiduously.

Elliott made up some story about visiting an "androgyne" who had been "castrated," and how this "case study" interested Crane the reporter as a "possible article." Of course, Theodore knew that nothing of the sort could ever be considered news fit to print.

Theodore became so anxious and consumed by jealousy that he could scarcely eat, or concentrate at work. He had never felt jealousy before, and didn't know how to leash it. For the first time in years he began to lose weight and his wife fussed over his health. She made it clear that she wasn't inviting him back to her bed but lingered with him in the sitting room after dinner. She even began to invite a few other couples to dinner on Thursday evenings, hoping to cheer him up, and she instructed the cook to enrich the vegetable soup with a good veal stock and to serve those Black Forest cakes the master of the house was so fond of.

One day Theodore happened to read a newspaper article about a detective, which inspired him. That very afternoon he headed over to Broadway on his lunch hour. There were a dozen firms, big and small, all within a few blocks of one another. He chose one at random that was on the third floor up a wide, shabby staircase. He didn't want to engage a celebrated detective, certainly not one who might have worked with the bank in sniffing out business fraud.

"M. H. Smith: Detective" was printed on the placard downstairs and, now, was stenciled on the door as he contemplated it on the landing. Inside, a man whose body was twisted like a corkscrew sat at a desk behind an iron railing and looked up with weary eyes and whispered, "Do you have an appointment?"

"No, I just—"

"Please be seated," the man, the secretary, said, closing his eyes as if to dismiss any further discussion and turning back to a brass nozzle, attached to a wide cloth tube, that he inserted in his ear. Two other clients (unless they were unemployed detectives) waited on straight-backed chairs. Close to the window sat a jaundiced woman in a neat if unfashionable dress with her cloak folded precisely on her lap, a mere excuse of a bonnet perched to one side of her graying head. And next to her sat a portly man with a bluff and hearty appearance who looked as if he were expending a full week's worth of energy just in sitting still. He was about to explode, Theodore thought.

From time to time a door to the left opened a crack and an undernourished call-boy squeezed out, whispered something in the secretary's free ear, and vanished back into the adjoining room. Even through the closed window Theodore could hear the rumor of Broadway—the rumbling carriages gliding over the smooth Belgian pavement, the warning cries of the reckless drivers, the ping-ping-ping of the trolley bells, the sudden upswelling of laughing passersby on their way back to work from a bibulous lunch.

Theodore tried to think out what he wanted to ask the detective, the instructions he wanted to give, but his mind was both agitated and empty, like a clouded-over night sky crazed with heat lightning. Sitting here with the shabby lady (did she suspect her husband was unfaithful?) and the foot-tapping hearty (was he worried his business partner was siphoning off all profits?) made Theodore alternate between bouts of tensing up and suddenly, disastrously, relaxing. The fits of relaxation undid him and made him feel empty in a new, horrid way, as if his head were glowing and his feet were melting away into a puddle.

The secretary ushered the shabby lady into the adjoining room. The hearty glared at Theodore as if he might essay to sneak ahead in line. Theodore longed for a newspaper. He recalled that the article he'd read had been full of dire warnings about unscrupulous detectives. Apparently some of the "sleuth hounds," especially in adultery cases, took money from both partners and reported nothing of substance to anyone.

When the foot-tapping hearty was at last shown into the office, Theodore was unaccountably relieved, even though he knew the hearty was the sort of self-important egoist who'd hold forth for a long time. Through the heavy oak door he could hear his shouting, as muted and vociferous as the calls of the vegetable man down below pushing his cart slowly up this grand boulevard.

By the time Theodore was invited to pass into the other room, he was so exhausted from waiting that he'd nearly forgotten the exact nature of his suspicions.

He was startled to see that M. H. Smith was a woman and a very young one. She stood and shook Theodore's hand.

"You can call me Margaret. Or Maggie. I don't need to know your name."

"I'm afraid there's been some terrible—"

"Because I'm a female?" She asked brusquely, laughing and sitting. "Cigar?"

Theodore waved the offer aside and said, "I presume a woman detective is hired, well, to trail female pickpockets or to spot lady shoplifters or to shadow women suspected of adultery—"

"—and your case involves a man?"

"A boy."

"Sit down."

Theodore did so.

"Tell me about your case."

She spoke with quiet authority, and her features, Theodore told himself, though not handsome were decidedly of an intellectual cast and honest, which could lead one in distress to confide in her.

As he thought these words he began to confide in her. "I'm, um, in finance and I have, um, a family."

"I won't need to know your name or anything about your profession unless it's relevant to the investigation."

Theodore was relieved.

He noticed that she was slender and carefully if soberly dressed. She was surrounded by devices for communication—a speaking tube that presumably connected her with her male secretary, an ink-stained blotter and a large green-cased Sholes and Glidden typewriter with its miniature amphitheater of pearly white keys and a sturdy-looking roller crowning it. He liked modern inventions himself and regretted that his superiors at the bank dismissed them as fads.

"Why do you want this boy shadowed?" she asked.

"He's someone I'm thinking of hiring at the bank. Though I have reason to suspect he might not be of the highest character. I'd like a report on his comings and goings and his associates." Theodore blushed since his lies sounded so transparent.

Maggie didn't blink. She took down Elliott's address and name and then asked, "Physical description?"

Theodore's heart started pounding and idiotically he said, "Yes!"

"What does he look like?"

"Oh. I see." And here Theodore blushed so thoroughly his cheeks burned. "He's small—about five foot six. He usually wears a newsboy's cap. In fact he is a newsboy, *dans ses heures*."

"I don't speak French," Maggie snapped aggressively.

"Part-time. Occasionally," Theodore said, chastising himself for using a French expression. He realized his whole story had just fallen apart—a newsboy would never be hired to work in a bank. At least a typical newsboy wouldn't have the good speech or self-effacing manners or clean fingernails or proper clothes to be a bank clerk, not to mention the honesty and integrity and slavish attention to detail.

Theodore looked at her almost pleadingly, as if she might expose him. "He has . . . beautiful violet eyes, soft skin, a beardless face, an . . . arresting presence."

"Well," Maggie said, laughing easily, "I'll find him anyway," which Theodore took to mean she'd seen through him and knew he was besotted with this boy with the beautiful violet eyes and that a lover's description was always useless. With just a hint of dryness she said, "When you first called

Elliott a boy, I thought he was a child, but now I understand he's a young man of sixteen."

"Yes," Theodore acceded.

"My fee will be ten dollars a day, and five days should be sufficient to map his comings and goings. Half of the fee is payable in advance. You may leave the sum with my secretary." She stood and shook his hand.

"Will you be following him yourself?"

"I might, or one of my operatives. Why do you ask?"

"Well, there might be some places he goes where a woman wouldn't be . . . admitted."

"Have you never heard of disguises? I'm a convincing young man in the right clothes and hat—convincing and, what's more important, inconspicuous. Good day," and here she nodded her head slightly. "Come back a week from now and you'll have a detailed report."

Theodore could not bring himself to leave just yet. His alibi now at last came to him intact: "This young man, Elliott Coolan, is my sister's son. She's the one with the beautiful violet eyes. I feel obliged to look after him and secure him a position at the bank. But in his adjustment period—"

Maggie laughed rather insultingly, brushed him aside, and said, "Don't worry, your secrets are safe with me." She opened the door and went out to murmur something to her secretary, who twisted himself about, looking for the appointment book.

That evening when he went to Elliott's house he had the uncomfortable sensation of being watched. He thought that if ever his friendship with Elliott erupted into a scandal the information that Maggie had accumulated about them could be used in court—or could it? Was there an unspoken confidentiality clause in the dealings of a private eye with her client?

A bright yellow forsythia was blossoming unseasonably in the patch of dun-colored garden below Elliott's window. Theodore was reluctant to drop the curtain and embrace Elliott, who was already undressing mechanically since he knew Theodore liked him nude. For Elliott these encounters must be dull by now, dreaded or tiresome, whereas for Theodore each time was the first. Like a lover who tears open every morning's letter with his temples throbbing and his mouth dry, Theodore expected to read something new and monstrous on Elliott's chest, in the softness behind his knees, in the elegant rigging of his bony ankles, in the down-covered space between his shoulder blades, in his violet eyes, but the message was always, astoundingly, the same: acquiescence, and even a mild pleasure.

Theodore knew that if he weren't paying the rent he would never have had this miraculous access to his body, and at first Theodore had accepted these conditions happily. There was an obvious discrepancy between them in how they looked, in how desirable they were—and in how much they earned. If an exchange of money for beauty redressed this imbalance, that was only fair, and reassuring. If Elliott needed Theodore's money, that meant he'd go on seeing him, undressing for him, performing these necessary duties. Theodore knew he wasn't strong enough to submit his love to the vagaries of chance or mutual desire.

TEN

CORA AWAKENED STEPHEN BEFORE DAYLIGHT. SHE AND THE doctor and two nurses had already had a nourishing breakfast of porridge and bacon and toast. Now they were all rushing about, getting ready for the boat to Calais. Even Spongie was cavorting; Stevie felt the dog's cold nose pressed against his own warm hand, which dangled just above the floor.

Stevie could see his wife was nervous. Her jaw was set, her hands trembled, she became impatient with the nurses more than once, which was so unlike her usual cool authority and composure. He'd seen her often in her Jacksonville establishment, where she received friends and important clients in her upstairs apartment at the bordello and sent the two black servants off to deliver ice to one room and clean sheets to another without ever interrupting her poker game or the stream of banter she was directing at soldiers who knew that any month now they might be shipped off to Cuba.

If this trip today had made her so tense, undoubtedly it was because she was afraid of killing off America's most famous young writer, Stephen thought. Her compatriots wouldn't forgive her.

Shaving and dressing irritated and exhausted Stephen. He was deliberately not cooperating; he knew that putting on his shirt and trousers was as difficult as clothing a corpse. He didn't raise his arms or even sit up straight. He couldn't. He kept crumpling to the left and falling asleep.

Like a field marshal, Cora had a dozen porters carrying their luggage and hampers down to the Admiralty Pier, where their channel steamer, the *Petrel*, was preparing to sail. After their room had been emptied nothing remained but Stephen himself, who'd been poured into a canvas chair that two burly men now lifted and carried through the halls and down the stairs.

The Lord Warden Hotel was one hundred years old, though quite recently it had been redecorated, it seemed, since the walls of the corridors had been paved over with Lincrusta Walton paper, linoleum printed with intaglio designs of Greek vases and garlands. The Lincrusta will be here a thousand years from now, Stephen thought, as he was being transported along by his two heavy-breathing stalwarts. Linoleum never decays. It alone is eternal.

Cora clucked and said, "Steady, steady," to no great effect. She kept battling her hat with trembling hands and skipped ahead of Stevie's chair. He noticed all these details—the designs pressed into the wall-covering, and Cora's anxiety, but at the same time, one moment swooned into the next with oneiric facility. His anal fistula sent shooting pains through his body, though he'd been given one of those new-fangled aspirins half an hour earlier; the taste of water had nearly caused him to vomit.

Near the front desk a bellboy was polishing the brass-plated entrance door and half-heartedly swiping at the boot-scraper. Cora ordered the stalwarts to lower the chair so that she might button up her husband's overcoat, tie his scarf, and pull his hat down over his head.

A cool mist, about to condense into rain, was sifting into the lobby—and then he was hoisted up again and was being trotted down steps through the mist and out onto the wharf and over the gangplank into the shiny black hull of the doughty little steamship. He was placed inside a private cabin that for some reason smelled of freshly roasted peanuts; by association he felt like a sick monkey far from his jungle.

After a last moment's scurry of returning French tourists onto the ship and a final clangor of bells in the midst of French laughter, the *Petrel* pulled out into the Channel. Almost immediately the boat was being swamped by high waves. Annie, the nurse, looked frightened under her big calico bonnet. She was swaying at the entrance to their cabin but after another moment of violent pitching she sat down on the edge of a chair and put both of her pale hands to her pale temples. "Oh dear," she whispered.

Dr. Skinner, still in his greatcoat, was trying in a very stagy way to be calm. "Yes," he was saying, to no one in particular, "we're never out of sight of land during this entire crossing. It's just twenty miles. Two hours or less. We're lucky it's a calm day."

It wasn't. The waves were coming at the ship from all angles like vultures already assaulting an animal that would soon be dead.

Charlotte, the other nurse, came back from a walk around the deck, her face wet from the heavy fog. "Ooh dear, I don't like that, they're all speaking French out there."

Dr. Skinner said, with a nasty smirk, "Well, that's what French people speak." And Stephen thought, It won't be so bad to be dead. He remembered that on the way to Cuba he'd been so excited he hadn't been able to sleep and had darted from port to starboard and back again, determined to see everything. That was just two years ago. Or two centuries.

Maybe he was remembering Cuba because his right hand ached—and for a second he could see all over again that moment at a dance bar in Havana when Jaime took a swing at a brute who'd pulled a knife on him.

I took the knife blow in my palm, Crane thought, which didn't seem heroic at the time, but Jaime, drunkenly, knelt and kissed my coat in gratitude.

Then back at the boardinghouse my hand became infected and blew up and I forgot to eat or drink water and all I trusted was tropical beer and if Mary Horan hadn't fed me with a spoon I might have died. I can still remember that when that big fat Irish woman would sit on my bed she'd tilt the mattress and I'd almost roll out. She must have weighed twice as much as I did even then, though she was no taller than I. Good old soul—she kept me fed and watered, and when I was better she made me go out every night for a walk. When I asked her to let me be, she said, "Upon my soul, you are the biggest fool on two legs." She lit a cigarette and said, "Ye are a damned little mambi." I never knew what that meant.

I suppose my muscles were in danger of atrophying. I wonder if that was the beginning of the end? Funny how a little thing, a knife wound in the hand, is enough to undo a life. As if all that is needed is a single break in the bodily envelope . . .

Dr. Skinner is heading toward me with smelling salts—I must look as if I'm about to faint. I do feel prodded at, like a dying mule the miners want to bear one more load of ore.

Ah! The smell of mothballs. I guess I did faint.

Now I'm wide awake. To what purpose?

Come now, Stephen, as my mother would cry, another little effort!

Dr. Skinner was saying, "Did you hear, Mr. Crane, that Sir Edward Reed has proposed to install metal tubes under the Channel? They'd be wide enough for the passage of a carriage in each direction. He claims the ocean floor here is very flat and is ideal for the laying of his tubes."

Cora was now murmuring, "That could be very good for Annie—I'm afraid she's being sick, Doctor, over the edge of the boat. Do you see now, Stevie? You're not the only one who's ill."

Stevie refused to smile; he let his face freeze in what he thought of as his Toltec mask.

The ship was bucking like a steer. Good, Crane thought. Even Cora is looking green. She'll be quiet now.

He went back to his thoughts of Havana. Mary Horan was old enough to be his mother. She was a resourceful old thing, even through the terrible food shortages, with her codfish salad. Oh, he'd infuriate her by not eating it, though he was willing to share a dram of rum with her.

When she made him go out for his late-night walks, he was never afraid. The whole of Havana was locked up tight and the streets were as quiet as those of a New England village, though occasionally he heard the muted riot of a tavern behind closed shutters that were leaking noise and light. He followed the Prado down to the harbor, where it ended in a filthy creek; there the cabmen washed their horses late at night.

Once he looked into a courtyard and saw black and white men hovering with sweaty faces over the strut and flash of a cockfight.

That was odd, pleasantly odd, in Havana—blacks and whites sat side by side on the train, or at church. One of the generals who led the insurrection against the Spanish was Negro—what was his name? Undoubtedly, they'll erect a coal-black statue to him, a statue made of coal.

Some of the male witches, those *brujos,* were Negroes as well. One of them lived next door to Mary's boardinghouse. Stephen had seen him in there, craggy-faced and flat-bottomed, in a nest of dyed feathers, sweet-smelling candles, and bits of tinsel. In his barred window, right on the sill, he had placed a statue of Santa Barbara; he offered a small orange to her every morning. Then he would fumigate his room by puffing on a cigar while he pushed a coconut across the floor with a broom.

Mary had a way of putting a skin on everything she said—the Irish in her. She'd say he was as serious as a Cossack. She'd call the policeman who kept searching her house for no plausible reason "a rotten little thimble-rigger." When she was complaining of inflation in the conquered city she'd say, "Soon we'll exchange a concert grand for a box of sardines." Stephen she called "the most hardheaded little ignoramus in twenty nations."

As the *Petrel* reared and plunged through the waves, Stephen inhaled the briny air. He could remember how raw Havana had felt with its smell of old hay and open latrines. Its Spanish grandees, fussed by defeat, were preparing to leave Cuba forever. He recalled the patrol set up at night by the American soldiers, who looked so tall beside the diminutive natives. They, the people of Havana, were intrigued by their new rulers; they translated the American Constitution and printed it on the front pages of their newspapers, as if it were hot off the press.

■ ■ ■

That whole time I was in Havana I was in despair. I would wake up shaking from malaria. When I'd look in the mirror, I'd realize I'd aged terribly—I'd gone from being a boy to an old man almost overnight. The more I became a wizened, bony chick, feather-less and shaking from the cold while I sweated from the heat, the more Mary Horan would hug me to her plush bosom, so firm, so plentiful . . .

Mary tried to interest me in a Cuban girl who lived upstairs from the male witch. She was pretty enough, but I'd always liked blondes. As a kid I used to say that if I ever met a friendly blonde, I'd marry her. Then I met Lily and wanted to marry her, though she was already married. She liked me, too. It was at Asbury Park among the Methodists, but even innocent pleasures can be wild. We turned that merry-go-round into a bacchanalia just by laugh-ing so hard. I remember I told her then that I wouldn't live long but that I wanted just to be happy for a few years.

A few years! What a greedy boy I was back then. Imagine even having one whole year of happiness, though at the time I thought my demands of life were modest. Lily didn't want me. She didn't want to run off with me, she didn't think I was handsome, even if she said she admired my almond eyes.

While I was in Havana, that silent, glowering city suddenly erupting into tavern brawls or cockfights or the ravings of the santero, as if the city wore a black cloak slashed with red—the whole time I was there, all I could think about was Lily, even if she never encouraged me. Mary asked me if I had a ladylove back home. I said I'd given my heart to a fair lass but she was already spoken for.

Crane remembered Lily, with her shiny-plaited hair, full cheeks, and deep dimples, her way of seeming a tomboy despite her married-lady dark dress with the wide embroidered collar that she closed with a pure white scarf, softly folded like an adoring man's touch around her throat. She was a good laugher! There was indeed something pure about her. Even though she said that she was happily married, for a moment there, back in Asbury Park, the night of the merry-go-round, she'd *almost* agreed to run away with him. He would have married her.

A year later he'd given Lily the manuscript of *Maggie: A Girl of the Streets*, but her husband destroyed it. Luckily the text had already been set in type and printed.

And just before he'd come down to Cuba he'd seen Lily one last time, in Washington. She'd agreed to meet him at the Library of Congress, there on the front steps in the sunny glare of white marble. Once more he blurted out his invitation—he asked her to run away with him and once again she refused him, though she hesitated, he swore, just a magical second before saying no.

As he plunged into and crawled out of dream-heavy sleep here midway across the English Channel, he kept thinking of Lily. He'd tarried so long in Havana because he wasn't ready to set up house with Cora. After all, Cora was married to a baronet's younger son, and she had no idea where Captain Stewart was living, nor could she divorce him if she couldn't locate him.

In Havana, Crane had written:

Thou art my love
And thou art the ashes of other men's love
And I bury my face in the ashes
And I love them
Woe is me.

Thou art my love
And thou art the beard

On another man's face
Woe is me.

Cora wanted to live in England forever and ever because few people over here knew of her past, but he, Stephen, wanted to be with her and didn't, was willing to live in England and wasn't, accepted the idea of marriage to her and didn't. Just before sailing back to England he'd changed his mind about Cora and England and looked for a bachelor's apartment in New York. His mentor, William Dean Howells, had begged him not to move abroad. "America needs you," he said. "England has enough great writers." For a moment Crane had even thought of living out West— exactly where, he hadn't decided (but he could sense as one might intuit a presence a white house in a cool morning light surrounded by mesquite trees and great nude mesas of rock).

"We're arriving, my Mouse," Cora said. "You're the only one who's still well among us. Look, there's the train station and the train is waiting for us and in a trice we'll be whisked off to Basel."

Stephen looked out and saw a château-like hotel growing larger on the right, and on the left stretched out the wide wood wharf. French customs was quick—duty was exacted only on perfume, tobacco, and spirits. He was hiding behind his Toltec mask.

He knew that Cora distrusted him ever since his Cuban disappearance and simultaneously loved him more furiously than ever. She knew about Lily—he had made the mistake of confiding in her.

ELEVEN

ALL DAY AND INTO THE NIGHT THE TRAIN REELED THROUGH the tilled countryside, past fields of sprouting hay and grapevines covered with pale-green leaves, through grim villages with their houses clustering next to a church like mourners around a coffin. The sky was milky and the houses the color of tea well diluted with milk. The air was cool when it was moving and sticky when it was still. Occasionally the train would stop in a town and the doors to all the compartments would bang open and vendors would walk alongside the *coupé-lit-toilette* compartments offering their wares, though murmuring, not shouting as they would in America.

Stephen felt his life force flickering, no more than a candle about to blow out, and his whole pained body hovered around this fragile blue light. His mind still registered odd details, and he knew his lips were working though no sound was coming out. His body was wracked with pain. Pain was all he knew now.

The day before they'd sailed Stephen had been visited at the hotel by two American writers, Robert Barr and Steward Edward.

He'd joked with Barr and said he didn't look natural without a cigarette in his hand. The doctor tut-tutted but Stephen, still whispering, had urged Barr to light up and while he was at it to bring him his pipe so that he could at least rub the bowl.

In front of Cora, Stephen had said gamely that he was feeling much better and looked forward to being cured in the Schwarzwald, but when she stepped out of the room to conceal the tears in her eyes, Stephen said to his visitors, "When you come to the hedge—that we all must go over—it isn't bad. You feel sleepy and you don't care. Just a little dreamy curiosity as to which world you're really in. That's all."

At last they arrived in Basel and Stephen was transported on a proper litter to the hotel Les Trois Rois right beside the Rhine. They went past a cathedral ("It's been turned into a Protestant temple," the doctor was saying in an aggrieved voice). Stephen's left lung ached at the back and when he coughed he felt his bones were about to break through his flesh. For someone healthy like Cora traveling was peaceful; she'd actually said she was sure he must find it restful on the train with the seats flattened out to make a bed. And now she was saying he was "terribly spoiled" being borne on his "palanquin" through the streets of the "historic center," whereas *she* was forced to walk over the wet cobbles with a hole in her shoe, letting in the damp.

She was partly playing the clown to keep up his spirits, but on another level she seemed perfectly sincere that he was somehow being indulged. Did she seriously not know how every movement stripped him of another erg of energy? As his world, once so vast, shrank to his cod liver oil, the constant buzz in his ears, the daily glass of milk he could never stomach, he fought not to be petty or fearful or resentful. She was this great strapping thing with the solid legs and firm breasts, the golden hair on top that was so tangled with life it constantly needed airing and even feeding—for she oiled her braids with linseed oil. How would she ever understand that he was a martyr to every step his sturdy Swiss bearers took?

"Yes, tomorrow we must go walking beside the Rhine," Dr. Skinner was saying, a bit short of breath as he trotted beside the litter. "This season is glorious in Switzerland, up on the hills, the white and purple crocuses are breaking through the snow and just now, before the fields are mowed, there are wildflowers everywhere. The blue gentian! How lovely it is, you won't believe the intensity of the blue, as if all the heavens had been condensed and purified into a single blossom."

Et cetera, et cetera, Stephen thought.

The next day he longed to get back to dictating his book, but he was too weak to move or even whisper. Cora raised him up to give him a glass of milk, but it tasted chalky in his mouth and so viscous when he tried to swallow it that he almost choked on it and finally had to chew it down.

He could see the look of fear in her eyes and he felt sorry for her. She complained about how dirty their rooms were and said, with a laugh, "I took the cheapest rooms way up here under the eaves, in fact we're in the maids' rooms and no one among us is taking meals in. These dirty little rooms cost more than the big, spacious ones in Dover. We've spent so far one hundred and fifty pounds on this cortège. They're very proud here to say the hotel was built in 1681, but I bet they haven't swept it out once since opening day." Here she stood by the small closed window, looking down. "The Rhine is lovely, Mouse, sparkling and rushing. I wish I could open the window but Dr. Skinner detects a slight weakness in your left lung."

"A weakness?"

She'd said it as if it were a nascent worry rather than a fatal reality. Oh, over the last few months he had been thoroughly immersed in the waters of euphemism—like the milk French women used to pour in their baths when they "received" in their tubs, a disguising milk bath of well-meaning double-talk.

He was shocked she'd used the word *cortège*. She meant "parade," but she'd chanced on the word for a funeral. He would have smiled—in his mind he did smile—but the effort would have cost him too dear.

As he slipped into and out of sleep his mind was awash with words and phrases—or were they turns of speech? As if language itself were a pattern book of carpenter's gothic, all the bric-a-brac of what could be said.

When he woke up the following morning he felt feverish but stronger or at least more focused and eager. Now he was far from England and unimaginably distant from America. Somewhere down there the Rhine was flowing swiftly under an old stone bridge, and in his future the Black Forest loomed up like death itself.

When he looked at Cora's severe, tailored traveling suit, beige with black frogs, and at her carefully dressed hair and her tired, frightened face, he was struck with the contrast. When he first met her at the Hotel de Dream (some of the other reporters had told him to go there, "If you want a good time . . ."), she had him brought up through the gilded and mirrored saloons to her apartment.

She knew who he was. She'd read him, she said, she'd read that *Badge* of his and liked it. Perhaps she'd only read the *Godey's Magazine* review, the one that looked at four of his books and repeated the absurdity that he was superior in recreating war to Tolstoy and Zola.

Right away he could tell that she wanted to be a writer. That he was supposed to represent art and noble ideals and spiritual uplift for her and her future as an authoress. He'd become accustomed to young women and even older women who looked on him as the heir to Edgar Allan Poe (he'd been called that, too, in the press), women who thought he understood them because he was sensitive, an artist.

He was willing to invoke the prestige of literature in order to seduce a woman, but it was a tricky thing. He didn't want to be idolized; that was too silly and it just made him burst out laughing. And he didn't want a woman to become so reverential that she forgot the body and renounced carnal desires.

He and Cora had stayed up late drinking after the other journalists had teamed up with girls or lost too much at cards and skulked off into the hot, airless city. Stevie had never met a woman who could drink as much as Cora, or "Mrs. Taylor," as she called herself. He failed to understand why she'd chosen that moniker. Her maiden name was Howorth, her first husband was called Murphy and her second Stewart. There'd never been a Taylor in the whole lot, but Taylor was her *nom de pute*, apparently.

They talked books. He gave her a copy of his *George's Mother*, a book he mildly regretted having committed. Too sentimental, with the poor old mum so battered and frail and courageous and the big lout of a son. *Godey's* had said the only good scene was the one where George first gets drunk.

They'd had a wonderful time in her big feather bed, as the ceiling fan turned slowly as a paddle wheel pushing them up the slipstream of the night. Cora had closed and locked her bedroom door, banishing her little world of laboring men and spoiled women.

He'd seldom felt so free with another human being. She was a

classy woman, firmly in charge of her establishment, but now naked and vulnerable in his arms. She shed years along with the stays
of respectability. In fact she became wonderfully companionable,
frank as a boy and relaxed as a sister. She put on his dress shirt and
wore it over her naked body as she got up to close the shutters and
to extinguish the oil lamp with the rose-red glass shade. She'd let
her bronze-gold hair down; it swept her shoulders. Under the
white shapeless volume of his shirt, her legs looked round and ti-
dily formed.

Tree frogs peeped outside and a sultry wind, rich with the
smells of night and the earth and stalled water, slid surreptitiously
through the slatted windows. On the crisp whiteness of her pil-
lowcase Cora reposed her head; all he could see was a point of
light on her teeth and a faint glint from the diamond chip of her
earring.

When he awakened in the morning, he guessed she'd long been
up. A maid brought him breakfast in bed and drew him a bath in a
big tub with claw feet behind an oxblood velvet screen that had
molted its plush in large patches. In a cage next to the tub a blue
and yellow parrot cackled to itself, said nothing and looked at him
quizzically, wrenching its neck from side to side, the better to take
him in. In a novel, he thought, it would symbolize Pure Curiosity.

Dr. Skinner begged Cora to go out walking with him in the fields
surrounding Basel. He was insensitive enough to say, "You may
never have another chance in this lifetime."

No sooner had the words escaped the doctor's lips than Cora's
eyes sought Crane's and she said, "No, I'll be staying here with my
husband. We have some urgent business to do."

Once the doctor had gone (he consoled himself by inviting

both nurses to accompany him), Cora brought paper and pen to Stevie's bedside and looked at him expectantly.

THE PAINTED BOY (*continued*)

Theodore longed to go out into the great world with Elliott. His love (maybe any love) needed to be walked like a dog, exposed to the adventure of the streets and the glances of strangers, permitted to mark its territory and parade its existence.

But discretion forbade excursions. Since they were forced to stay inside this room, Theodore took them on a trip into his past.

"My father was a banker, too," he said, as Elliott cradled his big, balding head on his naked lap. "Am I too heavy for you?"

"No," Elliott said. "Scoot up for a moment. There. I've rearranged the family jewels. Where'd you grow up?"

"In Cincinnati, Ohio. In a big brick house. My father was from back East. I don't know how he ended up in Ohio. Work, probably—on my father's side, I am a mixture of Welsh, Scotch, and English. My father's father had such a bad temper that his second wife (my grandmother) locked him once in the stable. He was so precise about written English that he'd correct every little flaw in his son's homework. He was suave and affable in public but at home he was irascible; he once beat my father for borrowing one of his hundred pocket handkerchiefs. My grandmother was Virginian, cultured and musical, although very undemonstrative for a Southerner. My father was six foot four and by nature sweet and considerate, just the opposite of his father. He wanted to be a university professor but was forced into the family business of finance. He greatly admired the man who was to become his father-in-law and waited for that man's daughter to grow up so that he might marry her. When they were finally wed, Father was nearly fifty and Mother just eighteen. He's been dead for a decade now, though Mother continues to live on in their house in Cincinnati near her sister and their children.

"My mother is cold and never loved my father. In fact she was in love with a rich businessman, also much older, and when he died she turned to spiritualism. I suppose she communicates with her dead lover through her damned séances. My mother wanted a boy and I was the firstborn, but she never showed me any affection; my little brother was her favorite . . ."

Theodore related his story in a firm, uninflected voice, almost as if he were giving an economic report, but as the tale became sadder, Elliott began to stroke his temples with small, cool hands—not with an irritating insistence but with light, occasional touches. He drew little circles on Theodore's skin.

Theodore went on. "I had a black nanny named Anna who was fiercely devoted to me. In fact she loved all kinds of children, and in her own little house, downtown near the river, she welcomed all sorts of strays—little relatives abandoned by their parents, but also unknown vagabond children. Anna was the only one who loved me, but her devotion could not compensate for my mother's indifference and my father's remoteness—I suppose he was remote because he was already sixty when I was ten and we had nothing in common. Or maybe we were both so alike, so reticent, that we just embarrassed each other. I never knew exactly what happened, but somehow he mismanaged the bank's affairs and he was edged out of his well-paying position. We continued to live in the same house but the cook and one maid were dismissed and if we traveled now it was in a second-class compartment. We had very skimpy meals, a chronic deprivation which has made me greedy as an adult."

Here Elliott reached around to pat Theodore's tummy through his undershirt, not mockingly or even comically but with respect as if it were a phrenological bump indicating the very quality under discussion.

"And I was a shy youngster, bad at sports, mediocre in my studies, except in mathematics, which I grasped so easily, so *quickly*, that I thought other people must be feigning incomprehension. I attended Oberlin College in Ohio. I appreciated the presence of female students."

"There were women in your college?" Elliott asked, genuinely surprised. "I thought they had their own colleges."

"Oberlin was a stronghold of liberalism. My father thought the students there were all anarchists and would have preferred Bowdoin in Maine, where there were no female students—but my mother insisted on Oberlin. I was graduated in 1875 and the tradition of abolitionism and women's rights was still very strong there. Before the Civil War, Oberlin had been a station in the Underground Railroad. In my day we had Negro students, and even one Chinese—not to mention some women."

"Did you ever fool around with other men in those days?"

"No," Theodore said, rising up on one elbow and turning

on his side so that he could look at Elliott, "I was very inno-cent and almost . . . simple, not in my studies but in my un-derstanding of the world."

"But I'll bet you *stroked doggy*?"

"Nocturnal emissions. In my dreams I was always in a melee of naked bodies both male and female, all naked. Let's not talk about this, it embarrasses me."

"Am I the first boy in your life?"

"Yes," Theodore said solemnly, "and only the second per-son. My wife, and you. But it makes me . . . anxious to talk about her."

"And who do you love more? Her or me?" Elliott asked.

He slid down beside Theodore, took his hand, and planted it on his bluish-white hip, as polished as marble.

"I think about you all the time. My feelings for my wife are sacred."

Theodore began to stroke Elliott's thigh. He was unhappy because tomorrow at lunchtime he would be seeing Maggie, the detective, and he felt guilty for having hired her to spy on Elliott and sickened in advance by what she might have discovered.

The next day at noon he walked up Broadway past all the most luxurious shops in the city—Sarony's, the fashionable photographer, Stewart's, the department store, Brooks Brothers, F.A.O. Schwarz, the Grand Central Hotel, and the various shops gathered into Old London Street, Wallach's Theatre and the Union Square Theatre. By night Broadway was overrun by well-dressed men and women and smart carriages drawn by spirited horses, everything illuminated by the glare of the fire signs in front of theaters. Below Grace Church, at Tenth Street, Broadway was dark, given over to imposing wholesale enterprises, all slumbering. Above Tenth Street and on up past Union Square to Twenty-third Street, the avenue was thronged at all hours and consecrated to the most elegant retail stores in the city—Lord and Taylor's and, on Eighteenth Street and Broadway, Arnold Constable's.

At Twenty-third Street the huge new Madison Square Garden with seats for five thousand people filled an entire city block and attracted throngs. It was said that the architect, Stanford White, lived in the Moorish Tower and entertained showgirls and society women in rooms gorged with the finest European antiques. Above Twenty-third up to Forty-second, Broadway was given over to the new theaters and the Metropolitan Opera House, which had been gutted by fire two or three years earlier and was only now about to reopen. Mr. Niedermayer, the bank president, kept a box there, not on Monday, the "social night," but on Thursday, a dim but solid evening for out-of-towners and minor functionaries. Theodore and Christine had accompanied the Niedermayers once to hear *Lucia di Lammermoor*. Adelina Patti had sung the role of the Scottish madwoman though she looked more like a Brooklyn mother of five and was already in her fifties. Reputedly, she had to be paid five thousand dollars in gold at least twelve hours in advance of every performance or she wouldn't go on.

Now, by day, Broadway was more subdued. There were few private carriages, though an abundance of hansom cabs jostled for room. In the shop windows well-dressed salesmen stood, their hands behind their backs, looking bored but convinced of their melancholy superiority.

Theodore was ushered almost instantly into Miss Smith's office. She was wearing an unseasonable straw bonnet trimmed with fake daisies and a large, blue, ill-fitting flour-sack dress. "I trust my disguise doesn't put you off," she said with a laugh and a firm handshake. "If you pay Mr. Reginato the rest of your fee on the way out, he will give you my report."

"Yes," Theodore said, confused by so much brisk information. He started to turn and head back out, but Miss Smith stopped him—again with one of her insulting little laughs.

She said, "I kept track of young Elliott for a week. I have a good idea now of his daily activities. For one thing, I know that he is visited every workday from five to six by a certain middle-aged banker."

Theodore laughed weakly. "I do go there every day." He hoped he wouldn't have to explain.

"In the evenings he sells his newspapers, usually in front of the Waldorf Hotel on Fifth Avenue and Thirty-third Street or near the southeast corner of Central Park, outside the Savoy Hotel or the New Netherland or the Plaza. The young man in question often wears female mascara and rouge, which catches the interest of certain well-heeled male clients, usually elderly. The young man has been observed at least three times entering one of the luxury hotels with a well-dressed grandfatherly type. I was able to tip a clerk at the Savoy in order to discover the identity of one such old party—a certain Mr. Bill Angel of Toledo, Ohio, owner of a local brewery. The fifty-cent bribe has been added to my expenses."

"Did he stay long with . . . Bill?" Theodore asked. He suddenly felt much too large for his clothes.

"Thirty-nine minutes. That was the longest appointment of the three. On Tuesday last I followed Elliott when he paid a visit to a doctor for venereal disease in a shabby neighborhood near the East River. He was accompanied by a small, badly dressed man in his twenties with flowing hair and mustaches whom later I was able to identify as a journalist."

"Stephen Crane?"

"Yes, that was his name. Is he well known?"

"No." Theodore paused. "Does Elliott have a venereal disease?"

"I have no idea, but if he is consulting a specialist I might be led to certain suppositions."

"I see."

"But perhaps you had specific questions?"

"Perhaps," Theodore said slowly. "Does he have any friends?"

"Yes, he sees a lot of a red-headed Irish newsboy."

"Oh, so they're friends?"

"Frankly, Mr. Koch, I have the strongest suspicion that they're thieves, a team of pickpockets. One of them distracts the victim—"

"—that would be Elliott—"

"—while the other one, whose name seems to be Mick or Nick, makes the dip, as they say in the business."

"Oh. The dip. That's what they say, do they? And are they . . . intimate?"

Maggie breathed out a scornful little laugh through her nose. "Of course I haven't observed them in privacy, but Mick or Nick did invite Elliott up to an expensive room in a hotel off Union Square where they remained for a little more than an hour. But Elliott's activities seem to have but three themes—your daily visits at five, his newspaper vending late in the evening, and his constant availability to men."

"Constant?"

"He seems to belong to a confraternity of very special newsboys. He made two and sometimes three deliveries on every day under observation to gentlemen in their places of residence—during which time he would remain for twenty, or at one time, thirty minutes. These deliveries were all in the early evening. For an extra fee, I can supply exact addresses. Of course he might have just been chatting or delivering something other than the paper, but given his general pattern, I would suspect that there is an elegantly simple solution to the riddle."

"Undoubtedly."

"I have but one question, Mr. Koch."

"Yes?"

"How does he do it?"

"Do what?"

"Where does he get the . . . stamina?"

"Oh. I see. I suppose he isn't required actually to do that much."

Theodore took a hasty, crestfallen leave, but as he was paying the rest of the agreed-upon sum, plus fifty cents in bribe money, to Mr. Reginato, Miss Smith, still wearing her absurd hat and country bumpkin dress, called him back in: "Would you mind just stepping into my office for one minute?"

"Not at all."

Once she closed the door again and they were alone, yet still standing, she said in a low voice, "There's something else I think I should tell you."

"Yes?"

Theodore longed for the anonymity of the street and the freedom to walk off a gathering feeling of oppression he knew could only get worse.

"Two days after your first meeting with me, a lady came to call, extremely agitated. It was your wife, Christine."

"Christine? But how on earth—"

"She'd found my card on your night table in your bedroom. You have separate bedrooms, I take it."

"And? Why was she agitated?"

"She told me she's had a growing fear that you're having an affair with another woman. When she saw my card, which you recall does not give my profession, she felt certain that I must be your paramour. Only once she came here to the office did she discover I am a detective. She said she was willing to pay my fee in order to pose certain questions about you, but I explained that I could not accept her custom since I was already in your employ. Unaccountably she seemed vastly relieved by this information. She immediately asked me if you suspected *her* of an infidelity and whether I had been engaged to find *her* lover—whom she hastened to tell me did not exist. I told her that my sense of ethics bound me to inform my client, you in this case, of the nature of her visit here—and of course I didn't confirm or deny her suspicions."

Theodore stared at his hat in his hands. "Do you think he and Mr. Crane are . . . also intimate?" Theodore blushed when he realized that he'd brought up Elliott with a simple pronoun and no name, as if he'd been thinking all along of no one else, not even his wife. And his question proved how abjectly jealous he was.

"Your Mr. Crane is a friend to women prostitutes. I can

now recall a newspaper item about him, in which he was threatened with arrest for trying to defend a certain Dora Clark at two-thirty in the morning when she resisted arrest for soliciting. He got on the wrong side of the coppers."

On the way back to the bank Theodore rode on the cable car heading downtown. It was so crowded that he had to stand. He glanced idly at a young office worker in a top hat that dwarfed his small-featured face and a coat that must have been made for someone older and stouter. The youth was respectable, which Theodore divined from the meticulous condition of his hands and the high polish of his shoes and what appeared to be a hymnal in his hands (the young man flipped from a page of music to quatrains of short lines—the verses, no doubt). Perhaps he sang in a choir on Sundays. He was going now to a rehearsal, or so Theodore thought. Theodore asked himself how he had strayed so close to the moral edge like a somnambulist—and now someone, Miss Smith, had snapped her fingers and he'd awakened, teetering before an abyss.

His right hand was in his overcoat and he touched his own belly through the layers of cloth. Was he syphilitic? He had no lesions or chancres. Perhaps he should see a doctor. Thank heavens he was no longer sleeping with Christine, though the idea he could never return to her bedroom now, not with this scourge, made him sad, as if she were receding farther and farther into the distance. He supposed he'd develop symptoms soon enough but they could always be passed off as something else—a skin rash, a wasting away of the digestive organs, madness: wasn't syphilis called the Great Imitator because it took on the protective coloration of so many other diseases?

He smiled. It occurred to him he was happy to share Elliott's disease.

Should he tell Elliott of his visit to Miss Smith? He really didn't have the right to demand that Elliott change his life. Not unless they lived together. Not unless Theodore was willing to sacrifice everything—his job, his marriage, his children, his position in the world—for the boy.

He decided not to tell Elliott anything. But if he went by his room this evening he wouldn't be able to hide his feelings. Better to wait a day. As he stepped down from the trolley at Wall Street he thought of the boy's naked body, his small black nipples and his tight rib cage, like hands closing around a firefly, or at least something pulsing with light.

At dinner Christine was wearing a dress of black imperial serge, full in the skirt and tight in the bodice, which was heavily decorated with jet beading. The black made her face and small hands look extremely pale by contrast. Her mouth kept sliding into a crooked little smile. She was wonderfully attentive and even cut his meat for him and scolded the maid for setting the table with a soiled napkin in his usual ring ("We really must get rid of such sordid little shortcuts," she said, as if the staff had invented the idea). She moved her chair closer to his and when the children, after their supper in the kitchen, came by to say goodnight, Christine prompted them: "Children, aren't we fortunate to have such a wonderful daddy?" They looked startled. Josephine concealed her embarrassment by hugging her father and running off.

In his bed that night Theodore wondered what Elliott must be doing. He was tempted to dress and run to see the boy, who was only about eight blocks away in Chelsea, though he doubted Elliott would be home.

He realized no woman had ever spoken as directly to him, as bluntly to him, as Miss Smith had done.

He dreamed that a friendly young doctor stopped him and told him the bad news. Without a transition the doctor was already operating on a tumor in his brain. He could feel the instruments scooping out the diseased tissue, soft and brown as overripe cantaloupe. When he woke up, much too early, he thought of going back to sleep and reworking his dream so that it would come out right. As a child he had done that more than once. After he'd dreamed that his brother had fallen from a high wall and been shattered into little pieces, he'd forced himself to doze off again; in his new dream his brother was mended and happy.

But Theodore no longer believed in his dream powers.

He wondered when and if the syphilis within him would manifest itself. The disease was like someone who was "it" in hide-and-go-seek; would "it" be discovered around the very next turn or start laughing hysterically when he'd open the door to the wardrobe?

He thought of the disease as a pact between Elliott and himself. But how could he let Elliott know of the pact if he never mentioned his paid spy?

He read through Miss Smith's typed report. It disturbed him to see those words hammered out in black ink on thin paper. He could imagine eyes other than his own reading the report. When the maid entered to light the fire in his room he hid the report under the bedsheets and pretended to be still asleep. As soon as she drew the door shut behind her he hopped out of bed and fed the report to the flames.

But what if that twisted Mr. Reginato kept a carbon? Or typed it on a fresh spool of ribbon which he had then pocketed and preserved for blackmail purposes? He could expect to receive far more from Theodore in hush money then he'd ever earn in that tawdry little office.

Theodore couldn't bear to look at his own face in the mirror after he'd bathed.

If he didn't confide in Elliott, then the boy would never know they were sharing this great adventure, this disease that was rifling through all the hidden places in their bodies and stripping them clean. When Theodore thought of his future as a syphilitic—half-crazed, open sores running on his body, his frame starved from the collapse of his digestion—he pictured Elliott with him, clinging to him. He would stroke Elliott's hair and it would fall out and remain in his hand.

In a terrible way this fantasy consoled him.

TWELVE

WHEN STEPHEN AWAKENED HE HAD TO REEL HIS MIND in like a hooked fish that had almost swum away. Where was he? Was it night or day? Was he alone? Had he slipped through some duct or tube into another world altogether?

It was night, the last watch, and dawn was still an hour off, he suspected. Wasn't this the time of the night—pulseless—when people just slipped away and died?

He could hear one of the nurses breathing heavily and once in a while smacking her lips as she slept in her armchair under a blanket, her head propped up on an extra pillow. She'd loved her all-day promenade and now she was sleeping like a child, maybe even tasting again the rich fondue the doctor had offered her and the other nurse.

She was a healthy, smug animal, and she looked on his illness as if it were an exception rather than the rule, something queer and other than the fate she would undergo sooner or later. She'd turned his pain and physical disarray into an aspect of her profession. It was her job, he was her place of business, he had a condition that demanded professional help, hers. He was a pretext for her livelihood, which she earned in her flatfooted, horribly English way—

He broke off, realizing he was succumbing to the sick man's resentment of the healthy and the young. He hated it when the nurses would give him a sponge bath by unwrapping, one by one, various parts of his emaciated body. He was so ashamed that they should see him in this state; he was not so much older than they— five or six years at most—but their profession, this horrid profession they had made of his body, obliged them to treat him as if he were eighty. If for one moment they admitted he could be an older brother instead of a grandfather, they'd be too frightened to bathe him and chatter away and gnaw on their sandwiches and write letters home and accompany the doctor as he went off gathering wildflowers in the mountains.

Stephen remembered the last time he'd seen the real Elliott. It was just fifteen or sixteen months ago. He had been in Havana and on December 28, 1898, he'd sailed back to New York. That day he went to McClure's and ran into Hamlin Garland, the man who'd convinced him years before to destroy his manuscript about Elliott. Now he could barely bring himself to shake Garland's hand, and Garland must have noticed his coolness.

Later, when he was down on Park Place, he noticed a newsboy wearing the very cap he'd given Elliott. He saw the boy had a disfigured face. Stephen studied him as the boy squirmed through the crowd, snapping a paper with a practiced flourish in front of one man after another.

The face had been burned almost beyond recognition. It was, in fact, a face that had been *effaced*, converted into a quilt of shiny red segments separated by raised, white welts, a lattice of glazed piecrust; his nose was just a melted bump and two black nostrils, his mouth a lipless gash. His eyes seemed to have been buried alive in this dead scar.

"Elliott?" he said, touching the boy's thin bony arm, which felt as hard as metal through the thin fabric of his coat. "It's me, Stephen Crane," he said, as if he were the one who needed to be identified. The boy just looked at him, raised his collar and tugged his cap down. And yet he was convinced he saw tears flood Elliott's eyes, the only points of recognizable feeling in his extinct face: two lava puddles in a burned-out crater.

When he'd seen Elliott's face, so soon after running into Garland, he took it as a sign that he should re-create the novel that he'd started and thrown into the fire so long ago. Until then he had almost thought that Elliott must have fallen ill and succumbed to one harsh New York winter too many. Or maybe he had been sent by one of those charitable programs to Maryland—those programs that relocated scrawny New York newsies and turned them into strapping, provincial farmhands. Now he saw that the boy had stayed here all along but that a tragedy of classical dimensions had overtaken him, as if the rouge and mascara he'd worn had ignited and burned his flesh to the bone like Medea's cloak. The blatant painful fact of his disfigurement demanded that Crane return to the story eventually and finish it. He now knew how the story would turn out, though the events leading up to the end needed to be filled in. Stephen had waited till the rest of the story had come to him—maybe he'd waited too long.

When Cora came in with his breakfast and a forced smile, he asked her to bring him a large café au lait, mostly milk with a drop of vanilla if they had it—he yearned for the taste of vanilla. "They should have it," Stevie said. "Vanilla sauce is the only thing in the whole German cuisine I like, and here in Basel, despite the French airs they put on at the front desk, Germanness rules supreme."

"It's wonderful that your appetite is coming back," Cora said.

He merely smiled. He knew it wasn't true. He just wanted a bit of energy in order to dictate. Wasn't tuberculosis supposed to make its victims restless and extravagant, incapable of repose, their minds on fire, their passions (even their baser appetites) unquench-able? He never felt lust these days—he seldom heard even the faintest echo of desire—but like Violetta in *La Traviata* he had an inexplicable phantom vitality coursing through him and galvaniz-ing his pitiful body.

He began to dictate, stopping only when Cora would moisten his lips with the milk from time to time. As he told her the story, he watched her face for reactions. Though keeping up with him was hard work, nevertheless an intelligent smile would sometimes flicker across Cora's lips in recognition of some irony or shred of humor he'd just invented. If he adapted something from their own lives, she'd glance up with a small stare of recognition.

THE PAINTED BOY (*continued*)

Theodore decided he must commission the statue of Elliott without delay. Knowing they were both ill with this most mysterious disease of all, one that usually roamed about slowly but that could suddenly pounce, made him want to freeze the moment and replicate Elliott's beauty.

Rather recklessly he sent a note via a messenger from the bank all the way out to the Bronx and the studio of the Pic-cirilli Brothers, Furio and Attilio. He had just seen a small marble statue of a laughing faun by Attilio, and he was convinced that the Italian maestro could do something along those lines using Elliott as the model. Secretly he hoped that the boy would be required to pose for hours and days on end, which would keep him away from all his other admirers. Of course Theodore would compensate Elliott for the hours he lost by not working—the "work" being defined in this case as vending newspapers, not selling his favors.

After a late-February snowfall and three arctic days, Persephone had decided to return to the land of the living from the cold embrace of the underworld. Almost overnight Mother Earth staunched her tears and smiled and Theodore Koch put his Chesterfield away, he hoped for good. Signore Piccirilli (it was Attilio who signed the letter with an artful flourish) gave them an appointment for the following Saturday afternoon. It was warm and the boy seemed happy to be out in the world with his protector. They took the elevated train to the Bronx, where they got off and found a cab that left them at the Piccirilli Brothers' vast studio on East 142nd Street.

There were three large new houses—one a residence for the Piccirilli family of stonecutters, apparently, and the other two studios.

"It's quite an adventure coming all the way out here," Theodore said with more bland equanimity than he felt. In the train he had been terrified of seeing someone he knew, not necessarily someone from the bank, but a friend of his wife, perhaps. He'd resolutely turned his face toward the window as if he were absorbed in the spectacle of the roofs of the houses and the distant glint of the East River. The river looked as if it were hammered silver, pocked by the wind, though a passing cloud dulled it to pewter. Some of the roofs were mansarded or level and gardened, but others were covered with asphalt and gravel; almost every roof was topped by a water tank of unpainted boards.

They scarcely spoke. Elliott had made an entire ritual out of bathing and washing his hair and putting on his new suit, the one Theodore had just bought him, as if he were going to be photographed in his Sunday best rather than sculpted in the nude. In his message to the maestro, Theodore had mentioned that he was bringing a young relative with him, hoping that Signore Piccirilli would accept to do a commission, a full-length statue of a small person in the nude—a "variation," he wrote, "on your recent dancing faun which I so much admire."

Of course the whole thing was preposterous and dangerous: a paunchy middle-aged banker asking an Italian sculptor to carve a naked statue of his "nephew." At the bank he'd even heard Mr. Niedermayer's insolent young assistant, Tom King, quip, "Did you hear the one about the two old perverts who meet in the street? One of them is with a rouged young man and says, 'Do you know my nephew?' and the other one replies, 'Yes, I do know him. Last year he was *my* nephew.'"

The story was such an assault that unwittingly Theodore had let his eyes search out Mr. Niedermayer's for reassurance but Niedermayer, fortunately, had interpreted the look otherwise. After guffawing, he raised his nearly translucent index finger and said, "Very droll, King, but hardly the sort of pleasantry that bears repeating to bank personnel." King bent his head in a show of pious repentance.

■ ■ ■

Now gray clouds were suddenly scudding across the sky. Soon it would rain, Theodore surmised, and he put an arm across Elliott's narrow shoulders as if his only purpose were protective, to hurry him inside.

They were ushered into a high-ceilinged studio by an assistant who was long on smiles but short on words in English. Theodore asked him a question but the handsome young assistant just shrugged and grinned helplessly. His hair looked powdered—oh, marble dust . . .

As soon as they were led up to the marble pile where the maestro was working, the assistant eclipsed himself with a funny little bow, a halfhearted wave of his right hand, and a rapid back-step. Piccirilli was holding a steel point in one hand and a lump hammer in the other; in a rather stagy manner, the sculptor was shaping the stone roughly and energetically, his muscular forearms rippling with the effort. A stub of a cigarette was held between his lips, casting smoke into his weeping left eye.

Having chipped away a long shoulder of marble, the sculptor, who looked to be about thirty, with his carefully trimmed mustaches, full head of black hair and pugnacious chin, let the cigarette fall dramatically from his lips to the floor as he turned to welcome his guests.

"*Scusatemi!*" he exclaimed.

"*Niente,*" Theodore said, hoping that was the right word. "It's nothing—we interrupted you, Maestro."

"Please, *s'accomodi, signore,* welcome, welcome, *benvenuto, anche lei, giovane ragazzo.*" Lots of smiles, though Piccirilli's eyes were small and sharp and taking in everything, traveling like an architect's to measure the possibilities of a new room.

They were led with many gestures and bows to a simple chair and an elaborate carved-wood couch covered with a tattered silk upholstery—something too fine for the studio. Piccirilli made a great show of dusting it off for his visitors. "You must forgive our marble dust—it is the sign of our work!"

"Of course, of course," Theodore said with embarrassed joviality.

"Now, let me introduce me. I am Attilio Piccirilli. My brother is Furio. We are from the great marble *carriera*—the qua—"

"Quarry," Theodore interjected quietly, not wanting to imply that English was to be preferred to Italian, the language he was supposed to be studying.

"Yes, the marble"—flicker of a smile—"Karrie of Carrara. We say *cava* for . . ."

"Quarry?"

"*Ecco! Cava* more simple, no? We are five brothers, and our father has taught us how to carve marble. When we come to *A-may-rica*, in 1888, the sixteen *Aprile*, we have no money. To eat we have to sell my trousers for two dollars. When there is a grand fire everyone run out of the building, saving me, I stay. Why? No *pantaloni*. Only long underwear. *Brutta figura. Fortunatamente*, our house no burn. Next day everyone give money to buy new trousers for poor Attilio." He mimed laughing uproariously but no sound came out.

He has told this story many times, Theodore thought, but it only works because he's telling it in this beautiful double atelier; it's obvious it is a rags-to-riches story. "Well, I'm Theodore Koch. I wrote you, and I want to commission a statue of my nephew here, Elliott."

"You are Elliott Koch?" the sculptor asked with a politeness that was a send-up of the slight contempt he seemed to feel. Perhaps he could tell from Elliott's bad teeth that he wasn't really Theodore's nephew but a pauper paramour.

Elliott just nodded and smiled. His eyes swerved from side to side as they did when he was ill at ease.

"And you want a portrait bust, *un busto*?"

"No," Theodore said, "we want a life-size nude statue, like your *Dancing Faun*." His own voice, he could tell, was quaking.

"I see," Piccirilli said, carefully, neutrally. "That would be a pleasure." A light came back to his eyes. "But perhaps you want an espresso, our very strong Italian coffee?"

"Yes," Theodore said. "Elliott?"

The boy nodded slightly, as remote as a Japanese princess.

After the maestro himself made the coffee on a gas burner and poured it out with a parody of Italian gusto, he led them both, cups in hands, into a smaller room with a door that the sculptor locked from the inside. *"Ecco!"* he whispered. "Now we are completely alone and *tranquilli*."

"*Sì, sì,*" Theodore said idiotically.

"When you have terminated your *caffé*, young man, *forse* you can . . . *spoliate*—"

"Take his clothes off?"

"Yes, *that*," the maestro said, pointing to Theodore, his most brilliant charade partner. Then to the *ragazzo*, "Unless you want to wait . . ."

"I will undress," Elliott said quietly but with a certain authority, almost as if he meant, *That's what I do best: undress*.

"I have some paper and pastels here," the Maestro said. "I will do some sketch first so that I know you body, Ell-yott-uh." The maestro pronounced *yott* with a deep, hollow *o*, as in *ottoman*, but he added the inevitable soft vowel after the strong double *t*.

Elliott stood, looking down at one shoulder as he slowly undressed, smiling as if aware of the effect he was producing.

"Good, this is good," Attillio said, picking up a large sketch pad that he propped on his knees and held at an angle with one hand while he drew with the other. "Of course the head is most important. Most difficult because, Ell-yott-uh, your *zio* want a likeness, no? *Somiglianza*, we say in Italian. The likeness come not from getting the eyes and lips right— that's what everyone think, no? But likeness come from getting forehead and cheek right. Cheek? *La guancia*?"

"Fascinating," Theodore murmured, half-wondering how this man, supposedly an adept of beauty, could chatter on in the presence of this miracle—this ordinary miracle—of spirit and flesh.

"Now turn around, *girati*."

With his half-smile, Elliott turned his back to them. There was a slight red waffling where he'd been sitting on a cane-bottomed chair just before he undressed. Theodore knew how sensitive his skin was. He could write his own initials, TK, on Elliott's back and a second later the red letters would be visible. His buttocks were placed high; they were so full that the crack between them was deep. There were two black moles on the right buttock, like peppercorns on white linen.

The maestro put down his pad and said, "Young gentleman, here, stand on this." He pointed to the elaborately carved base of a column. He offered a hand to Elliott, who took it and stepped up. "Now, put your weight, *il peso*, on your left foot—*sinistra!*"

Elliott did so.

"Bellissimo!" The maestro let his left hand lightly touch the flawless skin while addressing himself to Theodore, who could feel his own face turning rigid. "Look-uh, signore, most of the peoples stand on one leg—not both *ugualmente*. The left-uh leg push up and tip-uh the hip-uh." His small hand touched Elliott above the hip. "Now the other leg is bent-uh, *piegato*, and the foot? It turn out but not too much, *comunque*. The *centro di gravità*?"

"Center of gravity," Theodore prompted.

"That, yes, moves itself to the left." His hand touched the boy's shoulder blade. "Now, Signor Ell-yott-uh, look the right. *Va bene*. Now, this-uh form of body we call *contrapposto*—beautiful, beautiful, like Donatello, the *Davide* of Donatello."

Theodore wondered if Attillio was attracted to boys or if he was just an exuberant Latin. His hands were now moving lightly over the whole length of the boy's body. "We see the body is *geometrico*. The head is sphere, the neck a tube—" He was touching the various parts of Elliott's person, "and the rib cage, *le costole*, is an egg, no? And the pelvis, *la pelvi*, is a box—*una scatola* . . ." He moved back away from Elliott, like a surgeon walking away from the dressed-out cadaver and lecturing to the amphitheater. "Beautiful, the human body, no? *Geometrico!*"

Theodore thought that Attillio took a little too much credit for its beauty.

"Ebbene," he was saying, "now we be serious . . ."

He pulled out a pair of calipers and made notations as he

measured the thickness of the boy's head, the distance between his ears, the width of his body from shoulder blade to
breastbone, from buttocks to groin. With a tape measure, like
a good tailor, he discovered the length of his arms. After each
measurement, he jotted something on a little piece of paper.

He said, "When I see this large penis I have to laugh! I was
the youngest student at the Academy of Art in Rome, just fifteen—but! But! I was the most brilliant. Everyone say so.
One day our *professore* go away, was sick, *ammalato*, and all
ragazzini in the class go crazy—each make big penis in clay.
I refuse. I think it *schifoso*, disgusting, but then they throw
balls of clay at me and so to be a part of group I say, *d'accordo*—
and I make the big, big penis! *Gli altri*—the other boys—they
destroy their penis in clay when they leave, but I—like
cretino—I leave my big, big penis under wet cloth.

"That evening, *direttore* of our school take the Japanese
ambassador by our studio. The director say, 'Ah, here is work
of our little Attillio, *che piccolo genio*, little genius,' and lift the
cloth—and *ah Dio, porca Madonna*!"

Theodore hated this big-penis story and could scarcely
follow it, but he knew enough to ask, "What happened?"

"Disaster! Catastrophe! The ambassador laugh, the
director—*furioso*! He had me thrown?—thrown?"

"Thrown out?"

"Yes! *Buttato fuori*, from the *accademia*. And he made sure
I am excluded from all other schools. *Maladetto!* Then the
other student, feel guilty—they write for me to the director.
Even the Japanese ambassador write—at last I accepted again.
What a drama? What a drama! The *commedia del cazzone*!"

The story was so unpleasant that Theodore could only
smile weakly. The maestro flourished a hand once again

across Elliott's buttocks. With horror Theodore noticed that there was a lump in Attillio's trousers and a damp spot.

"*Ebbene*, young man—you may put your cloth."

Elliott began to dress.

The sculptor sat down beside Theodore. He placed the sketch pad over his lap and began to arrange it surreptitiously. "A marble statue is a very big work. Many days of work, many hours of *lavoro*—is it for your bank?"

Theodore was sure he could see a glint of malice in Attillio's eye. "No, it is not for my bank, it is for our salon."

"The *salotto*? *Simpatico!*"

"Yes," Theodore murmured. He half admired this Italian way of speaking in exclamation points, but it made him even shyer than usual.

They arranged a schedule and a price, the discussion interspersed with Piccirilli's assurances that emotion in sculpture is not expressed by the face alone. "The sentiment must be in the muscle and in the bone!" Theodore noted his skill in interweaving the chillingly practical and the ardently artistic.

Piccirilli launched into a long technical discussion of "pointing." Theodore couldn't quite follow but it seemed the maestro would first make a small model in clay, which would be "corrected" (the likeness?) and then cast in plaster. This cast would next be placed in a wood chassis and measured in a hundred different ways with rulers that worked in from wires that fell "true" because they had lead weights attached to the bottom. These myriad measurements were then enlarged by a factor of four or five and transferred to a block of marble. Rods positioned exactly were drilled into the stone to the appropriate depth, where they left black points there on the stone. Then studio assistants would chip away all the un-wanted marble and the statue would stand free—but covered with black spots, as if plague-ridden. These spots would only be eliminated by the maestro in the final polish.

As if the settling of the price (eight hundred dollars for a three-month project, half the money up front) were just a detail, the sculptor rushed on to say, "Usually we divide the work, *all* the Piccirilli brothers"—and here he counted them off, starting, in the European fashion, with his thumb—"Fer-rucio, Attilio, Furio, Masaniello, Orazio, and Getulio. But not this commission. No, this one I do in private."

And here the terrible Italian actually winked at him.

Theodore and Elliott returned to Manhattan by boat, the sidewheeler steamship *Morrisania*, which they boarded at Morris Dock. Theodore sat inside, reading his paper, while the boy paced the deck, looking across the Hudson toward the steeply rising, wooded shores of New Jersey. Theodore thought the sculptor was frightful, but he had confidence in his talent, or at least his skill, and appreciated the complicity that had been established among the three of them. Atillio could be counted on to render realistically every detail, even the careful part in Elliott's hair, though he'd hinted he might reduce the size of the boy's penis and eliminate all trace of pubic hair ("Not very *estetico*"). Theodore thought that eight hundred dollars wasn't too steep, though he paid just twice that a year to rent his family's big brownstone.

THIRTEEN

DO YOU LIKE IT?" STEPHEN ASKED.

"What's going to happen?" Cora asked. "I hope Elliott isn't going to run off with the awful Italian. By the way, I just approximated all those Italian words you were using—where did you learn Italian? I'll have to get someone to sort out the spelling if you don't . . ."

"If I don't survive?" Stevie asked.

"Well," Cora said. She laughed to herself and said, "I like it that you've made yourself into a character—you've never done that before. I noticed how benignly neutral Theodore is with regard to the boy's profession, and I don't mean selling newspapers. I suppose his tolerance is a reflection of your own." Then she sighed, rubbed her eyes, and said in a small voice, "Don't talk about . . . not surviving."

She stood and walked back and forth, her hands grabbing at her skirt and bunching the fabric. She'd taken her shoes off and was in her stocking feet—one of those American eccentricities that the British took exception to. Stevie himself had been criticized by Mr. Bennett for having his Greek servant, Adoni, shave him every morning. Bennett had sputtered angrily, "Good God, man, can't you shave yourself? I do—every gentleman I know does. I suppose somewhere there must be a few lazy pashas who succumb to the temptation to be shaved."

"Pashas?" Stephen had replied, good-natured. "But pashas never do—they're afraid of having their throats slit. Only the peaceful and the innocent dare to submit their necks to a barber, Mr. Bennett."

"Do you want to take a nap, Stevie?" Cora asked. She'd mastered her feelings and put on a new smile.

"No," he said. "I feel I have only a day or more to . . . go on. Forgive me, darling, I'm such a burden."

"Oh, Duke! You're not!" she exclaimed. In the last few months when she wasn't calling him "Mouse" she called him "Duke," in honor of his feudal realm at Brede.

"Every moment with you is precious," she said. And she began to cry. "Even if the moments are few." She drew herself up angrily and honked her nose into a handkerchief. "I hope posterity won't judge me harshly for dragging you off to England. Will they say your work suffered because of me?"

"Of course not, Cora. In England I wrote 'The Bride Comes to Yellow Sky' and 'The Monster.' They like me more in England. I've received my share of abuse from the American critics, but I'm neither a braggart, as they say, nor an egoist. I'm just making my simple little place and I can't be stopped—well, I can. By death. But not by the *Commercial Tribune* or *Munsey's Magazine*." He reflected for a moment and rubbed the bowl of his pipe, which he never smoked now. "England is a nice place to live. It's been good to Whistler and Sargent and James. And to us."

She ordered him some chicken broth and later washed his feverish forehead with a cool cloth. He wanted her to open the little window so that he might hear the sound of the Rhine, but she was afraid of a draft.

His eyes kept straying to his pocket watch, which he'd placed on the nightstand beside the bed. It was a classic French *oignon*, which someone had brought back from Paris for him. She knew that time was the one commodity in short supply and that he hated to waste a single unit of it. He'd drunk half a cup of the bouillon and now he was ready to continue dictating.

She said, "Isn't Piccirilli a real person?"

He laughed, "Yes. I wrote a newspaper piece on him once. He's a marble cutter—he and his brothers cut marble for all the leading artists, Daniel Chester French and all that lot. But Piccirilli did do all those 'laughing fauns' and 'boys with dolphins.' Most suspicious. You should change his name, though, to protect the guilty—I'm sure Piccirilli is guilty. It's obvious from his work that he likes men. Look at how he enlarged those buttocks of the sculptor in French's Martin Milmore memorial. Ha!" And he laughed at his own mischievousness.

She put her hands over her head and stretched. Then she sat back down beside him. She said, "I do like these odd characters of yours. You were never much good in catching women; I suppose an invert story was inevitable."

"What do you mean my women are no good? What about the heroine of *The Third Violet?*"

"What about her? You call her Miss Fanhall, throughout. She's as silly as all her friends. They're interchangeable nitwits."

"But—"

"Shh . . . don't splutter. Let's get back to our men. That's what interests both of us."

"But I love women!"

"I'm the last person on earth you have to convince of that." She winked at him. "Our men with the big equipment."

"Only Elliott! And that's—" He caught himself and laughed. "I was going to say that's how he really is. Cora, these chumps are so real to me."

"To me, too."

Crane closed his eyes. "Of course I knew Elliott slightly, but I never saw him undressed. When I think of *my* Elliott, the one in my book, I don't even picture the real Elliott anymore."

THE PAINTED BOY (*continued*)

Theodore made a serious mistake at the bank. He lent a furrier ten thousand dollars without demanding proof of collateral. The borrower, who'd not counted on the Panic of 1893 (the bankrupt railroads, the armies of unemployed, the failing banks out West), was suddenly unable to sell his minks, or even his Persian lambs. His business went under and his stock, and even his personal belongings, were seized and auctioned off, bringing in only ten cents on the dollar.

Theodore could scarcely remember the transaction; like almost everything else it was obscured by the magic-lantern pictures in his mind of Elliott by the window, Elliott on his lap, Elliott's face contorted with the pain of pleasure, Elliott pacing the deck of the *Morrisania*, Elliott nude being handed up by the maestro onto the base of the Corinthian pillar. Theodore himself had had to take a loan for five hundred dollars, placed into a special account so that his wife never had to know of the transaction. He needed the money to pay the first installment of Piccirilli's fee.

Mr. Niedermayer asked Theodore if he could step into his office for a moment later that afternoon at four-thirty. Theodore smiled and said, yes, of course he would, but his first thought was that he would miss one of his usual rendezvous with Elliott. He recognized the gravity of the precise appointment lurking under the studied casualness of "step in" and "for a moment."

He wondered if he'd lose his position. And again all he could worry about was finding the money every month for Elliott's rent. He'd heard of addicts, opium addicts; was he addicted to the boy's body? Throughout the day, during its rituals and its tedium, he felt as if he had a melody in his head drowning out all of this noise. The vision of the boy's white body, as white as the snowiest block of costly Cararra.

Mr. Niedermayer met him at the door of his office and ushered him to a chair. "Sit down, sit down." He himself sat on the edge of his desk, not far from his employee. "Now, Koch, I don't want you to feel bad about this . . . miscalculation. We all make our miscalculations, don't we? That's how we learn, isn't it? Through making miscalculations." Mr. Niedermayer had acquired the British habit of adding an interrogative to every sentence, one that required nothing of the other person except mute assent.

"Yes, absolutely, Mr. Niedermayer," Theodore said, feeling as if the objects around him were being looked at through the wrong end of a telescope.

"What does worry me, Koch—" And here he broke off and asked in a strangely timid way, "We do know each other well enough, don't we, for me to call you by your last name?"

"Of course. We've known each other for seventeen years." Theodore didn't want to sound ironic about all those years, or reproachful—nor did he want to use a name, since he always called his boss "Mr. Niedermayer" and didn't think it wise to point up the disparity in their differing forms of address.

"Well, Koch, yes, of course, we go way back, don't we, and you've always been one of my most reliable, uh, standard-bearers, haven't you." This was intended as a pleasantry and Theodore smiled. "But recently the flag has been drooping, hasn't it, or the soldier has been daydreaming, if you catch my drift. I can recall the time when you worked every day late into the night and you were always here before everyone else, but now you always take your leave, don't you, at fifteen minutes before five? Please don't think we're keeping track or that a minute here or there matters when we're dealing with a respected bank officer like you—no, it's just, possibly, a *symptom* of a deeper problem, if you catch my drift."

Theodore was thinking that perhaps he could move his rendezvous with Elliott back an hour every day to six, but then the boy would have even less time to sell his evening papers, and Christine would have to hold the dinner to eight. This would cut into his playtime with the children.

But Theodore knew that he was being placed on probation and that a fired banker would never find a new job these days.

Mr. Niedermayer was saying, "Of course the public is very alarmed by all the recent banking irregularities—and the outright fraud of the bankers. Naturally in your case we're only talking of a slight misjudgment, aren't we. But we mustn't present our stockholders or the general public with the least cause for uneasiness. In one of our neighboring banks, which will remain nameless, the president would serve himself with as much as fifty thousand dollars in cash and say, carelessly, to the clerk, 'Put a memorandum in against me.' In Philadelphia the president of a bank, in collusion with his clerks, took a round million out of the failing institution."

Mr. Niedermayer droned on, piling up other examples of recent fraud; he even mentioned one bank president who *was* the bank and who robbed the tills so systematically that he had to kill himself to escape disgrace and punishment.

As Niedermayer lost the train of his thought (he seemed intensely uncomfortable), Theodore began to wonder how easy it would be to bilk the bank out of a fortune. What would he have to do to rob the tills not of pocket change but of real money? Not that he'd ever pocketed a dime up till now.

He didn't want to be caught. He'd have to make sure he didn't suddenly start living extravagantly.

"Perhaps you're preoccupied, Koch. Perhaps you're going through some domestic crisis. Or maybe you're undergoing a rough patch with your health, though I must say—" And here he tapped his own stomach and glanced down with a comic, pursed lip look of surprise: "We both *do* look as if we're flourishing!"

At last Theodore spoke, in a calm voice, respectful, but as if nothing were out of the ordinary. He said, "No, there are no crises! Everything in my life is in tip-top shape and remarkably ordinary. If I made a mistake with Feldman it was simply because he had taken out three previous loans—small ones, to be sure—and had always promptly honored his debt." Theodore felt as if someone else entirely was speaking in his stead but doing a good job of it. "As a result, I was a bit too casual about extending this loan. In the future I will be more rigorous about evaluating each loan on a case-by-case basis."

Here Mr. Niedermayer looked even more uncomfortable. "Well, regrettably, the board has asked me to move you out of loans for the moment and put you back in daily accounts."

Theodore didn't mind. He had to order his shoulder not to shrug, not even the least bit.

"We will present this whole change as a promotion, won't we," Mr. Niedermayer said. "You'll be vice president in charge of current accounts. After six months successfully at that job, we'll move you over to estate planning or something juicier. For the moment your salary will be unaffected by this, uh, *lateral* move."

Theodore intuited (hoped) that his interview was drawing to a close and stood.

Mr. Niedermayer pushed off from the edge of the desk, where he had been dangling his long thin legs, for if he had a big belly, his limbs were not fat at all. "You know, Koch, I find all this damn awkward—we've been associates for . . ."

"Seventeen years?"

"Precisely. And you're one of my most trusted colleagues."

They shook hands. Niedermayer's was all bone and breakable.

Theodore sent a messenger from the bank to Christine telling her he had to stay late and not to keep dinner for him. On the Ninth Avenue elevated train he rushed to Elliott's room on West Twenty-second Street. The boy was about to go out on his newspaper route but he relented when he saw how desperate Theodore was.

"Yes, come in. Close the door. How is my Duke?"

Theodore said that everything was fine, that nothing ever changed in his life, that he was just as steady, uninspired, and dully perfectionist as ever, but that he had suddenly panicked. He'd been held back by the unannounced arrival of a preferred client, one whose name was so august he couldn't reveal it. Theodore added that to head Elliott off. As a newsboy, Elliott knew almost all of the important names in New York and sometimes spoke of the illustrious in a familiar way—"Pierpont" he'd say for J. P. Morgan, and "Consuela" for the young Miss Vanderbilt.

"I'm thinking of installing a telephone here in your place," Theodore said. "Last week I visited the main office of the Metropolitan Telephone and Telegraph Company down on Cortlandt Street—all the officers of the bank were invited. Mr. Niedermayer is very suspicious of telephones but there are thousands of such subscribers in New York. At the headquarters there's a single unbroken switchboard that wraps around on three sides of the building—it's about two hundred and fifty feet long. And there are almost one hundred and fifty operators during any one shift. For some reason almost all the calls in New York are made between eleven and noon and between two and three."

"Hush," Elliott said sweetly. "Undress me. Hold me." Perhaps he wanted to be unusually attentive to his protector, who he could see was shaking with anxiety. Or maybe Elliott was just buying time. Theodore speculated that much as Elliott might think that it would be fun to possess one of the first telephones, he might not want to be at Theodore's beck and call at every moment of the day and night (did the thing even work at night?).

Theodore kissed the boy's naked body feverishly. He breathed in its aroma, inhaling deeply as if it were the bouquet of a great wine. He swirled the boy's cut-grass and tar-soap smells in the snifter of his mind.

Today he'd been called to account for his slipshod work of the last six months—and he gloried in the young man who had driven him to distraction. Now he thought this perfect, small body truly was like a drug, one on which the addict becomes more and more dependent and which must be administered in ever larger doses to obtain the same effect.

And just as the drug is a poison that the confused body perceives as a life-giving necessity, in the same way Theodore knew Elliott would be his downfall. Yet his only desire was to hold him and kiss him, to squeeze him so hard that they would become one person.

He appreciated that Elliott's demands were so modest, since otherwise Theodore was prepared to go so far as to steal from the bank to fulfill his whims (Elliott had no whims). "Put in a memorandum against me," a corrupt banker had said—according to Mr. Niedermayer—as he emptied the tills.

Theodore's passion had not become general, he had not sensitized himself to the appeal of other young men. Rather it was narrowing to a diamond point that traveled along the grooves incised in Elliott's person, as if on one of those new seven-inch recording disks a Mr. Berliner was propounding. Theodore never looked at other boys, nor women. In a strange sense he was faithful to Christine and Elliott both, utterly faithful. And his love widened only to include his children.

If what he felt for his family was esteem and the obligation to protect them, that sentiment was overshadowed by this passion—cruel, unstoppable—for Elliott, a feeling, he might say, that dwarfed the boy himself. It was as if Elliott's timid, somewhat secret, personality were just the frail ambassador appointed by the boy's body, this ruthless despot. Elliott's body was his true self. When Elliott was in the throes of desire, feeling its aching sweetness, its insatiable appetite, then Elliott the friendly, whipped farm boy would glance down, amazed at what was happening to his body, incapable of understanding its devastating power.

Theodore was proud to sacrifice everything for love. Growing up in Cincinnati with its arctic winters and swamp-heat summers, with his frigid mother and ancient, frustrated father, he'd been happy to play alone. He had had no friends, nor had he missed them, since he'd assumed other children were as solitary as he was. He knew nothing about comradeship. He had his imaginary playmates—a sensible boy, a bossy girl—and his submission was unquestioned to the tedium of a house at the end of the lane where the loudest noise was the tick of the French clock on the mantel.

At Oberlin he'd made friends with his roommate and the boy across the hall, but most often ate his supper alone with a book.

After graduation, Cousin Edna was ailing and Christine was living with her and nursing her. He'd met Christine in New York only by the greatest good fortune through Edna, a relative on his mother's side. He'd just returned to New York after nine months spent in Paris.

Christine's first husband had died in a swimming accident when he was thirty and she twenty, after only a year of marriage. She'd been in deep mourning for the past two years and had told him that she intended on staying faithful to Ralph Sutter's memory. She described him as an Apollo, though in the studio photograph she'd showed him he had a short upper lip that revealed a rabbity toothiness and a deeply eroded hairline.

Christine had only a small dowry (her father was a Presbyterian minister); her first husband had left her nothing. For the longest time Theodore feared he'd never be able to measure up to Christine's memories of Mr. Sutter, but he had soon become her best friend, and she his.

Because she was a widow she enjoyed much more freedom than an unmarried girl of her age and class would have known. They took long walks up Fifth Avenue on Sundays to see the mansions of the rich and the smart hotels. In fair weather they spread out a cloth on the grass and ate a picnic lunch in Central Park that Christine had prepared. Sometimes Theodore was invited to his Cousin Edna's for dinner and there, as if by chance, he was always seated next to Christine.

Once she told him that her only regret was that she had not had any children. He had said, "But, heavens, you're only twenty-two! You can remarry if only for the sake of bringing children into the world. I myself hope to father children, but not to have them raised by a nurse or nanny, as I was. Much as I loved my nurse Anna."

Once this interest in a family was shared, Christine and he often talked around the subject. They pooled their ideas. He hoped to have four children. She contended she'd be happy with just two, an older boy and a younger girl. They both considered Sunday school a useful method for imparting a strong moral sense to children, though they both abhorred fanaticism and enthusiasm. He rather hoped his son would prove to be scholarly or scientific; his daughter he'd like to study music, the voice and the piano. He said he believed that there was nothing more agreeable than a woman who could accompany herself, knowing perfectly well that Christine was just such an accomplished musician.

As they talked about these putative children, they ascribed to them qualities they esteemed in men and women—as it turned out, the very qualities they each possessed in the other's eyes. Christine wanted a boy who'd not be pushing or loud or competitive but steady and quiet. And Theodore thought the nicest girls were the old-fashioned kind who knew how to do embroidery and avoided every extravagance but could supervise and instruct servants and keep the household books. Curiously, Christine was already managing her ailing friend's household and was an expert needlewoman.

One day during a stroll around Washington Square (Cousin Edna lived nearby, on Twelfth Street), Christine confided in Theodore that her husband, though a saint, had had a nasty temper and one unbecoming habit: that of berating servants. "Of course he was a wonderful man," she said, looking away, "but he was impatient."

Perhaps he was deluding himself, but Theodore imagined that if Christine had conceded that her Apollo had had feet or at least toes of clay she'd done so in order to encourage his suit. She'd judged correctly, if that indeed had been her strategy; Theodore knew that he was patient and peaceful and elaborately polite in his treatment of staff. He gathered courage in wooing her.

They had married a year after they'd met. And early on

they'd discovered a corresponding deep reserve in each other. Christine had betrayed no sign of pleasure in making love and once a month had only vaguely lifted her nightgown to suggest she might be receptive. She was eager to have her two children and she bore a boy and a girl with unexpected fortitude. Her mother traveled down from Albany for each lying-in and had remained with them each time for a month.

The children became the unique subject of the young couple's conversation and the source of all their joy. Christine pleased Theodore by not handing them over to a governess; she kept close watch over them, nursed them when they were ill, taught them to read, and made Josephine play scales on the piano. By the time she was seven the child was doing exercises from Czerny and performing simple pieces by Clementi.

Theodore returned home to the house on West Sixteenth Street (just four blocks north from Cousin Edna's and six blocks south of Elliott's room—and two long blocks east). It was only nine in the evening yet the sitting room was empty and only a single gas lamp was lit. He looked at the comfortable armchairs, the drawn curtains and drapes, the good Turkey rugs scattered across the gleaming wood floors, the tiles around the fireplace decorated with little crabs and stars. Everything was tidy and cozy and a small fire crackled on the grate.

The Irish maid, who looked exhausted after her long day, came in and bobbed a curtsy. He'd asked her to give up that undemocratic habit. Now, to prove his point, he bowed solemnly back to her. This he instantly regretted since, wild-eyed, she fled the room, only to return with his supper, which she carried into the adjoining dining room. There she lit a lamp on the sideboard, poured him a glass of water, and whispered, "I hope it's not cold, sir." To which he replied, lightly mocking her, "Never fear, madam." The unexpected form of polite address made Mary (that was her name, wasn't it: Mary?) blush and hurry away.

He ate his chop and puree of potatoes and the overcooked green beans, which had turned a nasty khaki color.

The stairs creaked and suddenly Christine appeared. "Is it edible?"

"Fine. It's fine." He stood and kissed her on one cheek. She was doused in that lovely girlish scent of hers, honeysuckle.

"Please," she said, drawing him back down to his meal. She perched at the very edge of a chair. "Was there anything wrong at the bank? You never tell me."

"No, our bank is very sound, and now the Crisis is almost over. It was all the fault of that Sherman Act, and there was the terrible run on gold, but now our reserves are creeping back up. Most Europeans withdrew their investments, but now, slowly, they're coming out of hiding. The United States, all forty-four of them, are just too boisterous and go-ahead for financiers to ignore."

"So patriotic," Christine whispered with a little crooked smile. She patted his hand. "You do seem anxious, Ted." She couldn't bring herself to look at him.

He was tempted to tell Christine just a bit about his talk with Mr. Niedermayer, but he didn't dare. She was the angel of his hearth, the mother to his children, the downy, sweet mama bird nurturing his chicks. It would only be selfish to upset her, especially since the problem was one he'd created.

"Ted?" she said, and he stopped chewing, because she never once in the whole time he'd known her ever called even such a tentative halt to the normal flow of conversation or ever introduced an unexpected topic. "You know, don't you, that you and the children are the very heart of my whole world. There was never another man before you except Mr. Sutter, nor is there one now, nor will there ever be anyone else. You're my one and only." He realized she thought he suspected her of an infidelity. And these suspicions of his (according to her theory, he surmised) had caused him to make mistakes at work. He'd grown confused at the bank because he worried about their marriage—that's how she must see it all. Her determination to alleviate his baseless fears had caused her to take this extraordinary step of addressing his doubts in no uncertain terms. All of her theories, of course, were linked to her visit to the detective.

"I appreciate that, Christine," he said as solemnly as possible. In truth he felt all the more guilty since she assumed he was entirely innocent, whereas he was the one with the lover—he was the one who'd never sleep with her again even if she desired it because he was probably infected with syphilis. "Mr. Niedermayer wants us all to work longer hours at the bank, so I'll be taking my meals late every evening, which is a nuisance for you but must be done."

She nodded. She never complained about the inevitable. "Will you be giving up your Italian lessons?"

"Yes." He smiled. "I'm afraid I have no gift for languages."

"That's not true. You speak a lovely French, all from that one year you lived in Paris."

"Nine months, rather."

"Well, nine months," she conceded. "When we first met, you were just back from Paris. I'm surprised that silly bank has never benefited from your marvelous French."

Theodore smiled. She often commented on the bank's failure to profit from his French. The umbrage she took was a repeated little exercise to establish how much she esteemed him.

The next day on the way to work as he descended from the El he was caught up in a dirty, angry crowd of unemployed and unbathed men. One of them deliberately jostled him, but what shocked Theodore the most wasn't being shoved but the man's face: the intelligence and indignation in his eyes. His wasn't a humble vagrant's face, bloated from drink, brutalized from years of begging. It was the bright, modern face of someone who could be a colleague at the bank, a face he might see at his own table above the banked candles. With a sudden revelation, Theodore understood that this man was one of the recently fallen—it was like Dante seeing his own teacher from Florence among the dead. But Theodore wasn't armed with Dante's smugness, and he knew that the same thing could happen to him.

That was the terrifying thing about Manhattan. The castles of the multimillionaires lining Fifth Avenue were just blocks away from the little neat homes of the contented poor and the pestiferous swarms of the dangerous classes. At Five Points there was so much crime that the police would no longer dare to patrol the streets—and a cab, much less a private carriage, was never seen there. In fact the streets were impassable. Gangs of violent, ragged boys clubbed each other and controlled block after block. The Irish fought the Italians and both tribes fell with fury on a Negro who might stray onto their turf.

No hope. No hope for any of them. The women lived in their rags on the sidewalk, the children didn't even know the names of their brothers and sisters, and everyone, even the children, drank pints of beer. Many of the men had given up and sat in pubs all day and night hunched over their steins, their faces ravaged by alcohol, their teeth missing, their moods alternating between sullen defeat and violent rage.

When Theodore looked at these men he could transpose himself easily into their lives. He felt his own features thickening, his hair drying and falling out, a fish-belly fat encircling his waist while the flesh melted away from his arms and chest.

Once he asked Elliott what he thought about the poor. The boy laughed and said, "But I am poor. You've spoiled me by taking me in from out of the cold. But what will happen to me if you get tired of the Magic Flute? Boo-hoo!" And here Elliott mimed weeping and rubbing his knuckles into his eyes. He liked to joke around about serious things, to pretend he was feeling the very sentiments he was actually experiencing.

Theodore realized that every time he embraced Elliott the boy tensed up, perhaps because he'd been beat and buggered as a child. Had he grown addicted to violence? Did he miss it? Or was he looking forward to the day when he would be rich enough to mistreat a little sidekick of his own? Theodore wasn't sure he understood how any of this worked, but he was certain that unvarying affection must seem a bland diet indeed to the boy.

Unless Elliott was in love with him. But that possibility had never crossed Theodore's mind.

The following Saturday Elliott made the trip alone to the Bronx. He was scheduled to pose nude for the maestro on four successive weekends in sessions of three hours each. Theodore, of course, never saw his protégé on Saturday or Sunday, but on Monday (at the new hour of six, not their habitual five) he asked him detailed questions.

"Was he friendly?"

"Oh, yes. Very nice. He gave me a Bolivar without me even telling him that's my favorite. And a glass a milk, as if I was—"

"Were—"

"As if I *were*? *Were* a little kid? Although it's warm out in the sun, in his studio it's still chilly, and Mr. Willikers shrank right up."

"Mr.—! Oh, you really are a little kid. Did he touch you?"

"Just to get me into the right pose."

"And mood. I see. He might've explained in words what he wanted."

"You know how bad his English is."

"So there was a great deal of trial and error in arranging the *contrapposto*?"

Elliott smiled sheepishly. "Yes."

"You were alone, I take it. He locked the door, I suppose."

Elliott hesitated a moment, then said, "Yes, he locked the door but no, we weren't alone."

"Who was there? His brother Furio?"

"No, a man about thirty named Johnny Presto."

"An actor? That's a made-up name: Johnny Presto! Or a jockey?"

"No. He seemed to be in business. He was dressed in a dark blue suit with a thick gray line in the wool and another thin red one. But he didn't speak very good English."

"Was he handsome?"

"I never know what that means exactly."

"Come now."

"No, I'm serious. I always wait to see what other people will say. Anyway, yes, I suppose he was . . . were?"

"Was."

"He's handsome, though he'd make an ugly woman with his big nose, thin lips, and ears that stick out. But he has slicked black hair and a nice smile and small eyes, *intelligent* eyes."

"Did he touch you, this Mr. Presto?"

Elliott said, "Just with his eyes. He was there to discuss business with the maestro, but not sculpture business. Something to do with Italians and the funeral parlor business. He wants Piccirilli to make the alabaster vases that stand outside on the street. He wants them lit from within by electric light-bulbs and he wants them cemented in place so no one's not gonna heist them."

"Steal them. So no one will steal them."

"I'm only telling you how he said it."

"What else did he say? Did he talk pretty to you?"

"He offered to drive me to Manhattan in his carriage."

"Did you accept?"

"No." Elliott lowered his eyes. "After he left, I asked Signor Piccirilli about him. He said Johnny was from Kansas, that his father had fought for the South and lost everything. He said Johnny was rich and getting richer by the day."

"I'm sure that he's from Sicily, not Kansas. And that his

father fought for Garibaldi. These Italian criminals are in the news. That must be how Piccirilli knows him—they're both Italians. I'm sure he manages crime on Mulberry Street. Most of the criminals in New York are Irish or Jewish, but the Italians are starting to come to the forefront." Theodore paused. "I suppose Piccirilli asked you about me? Whether I'm really your uncle. Whether I'm rich and getting richer."

"I told him we're related but through marriage, not by blood because, Ted, we don't really look that much alike, and you being so refined . . ."

"No, that was good. And?"

"I remembered you told him you were a banker, so I just repeated that. I started to tell him about my dad's farm and my ma's death but he wasn't really interested, I could tell."

Theodore wondered if the artist would end up by making love to Elliott, or was his game to play the pimp?

Elliott said, "Maybe you're right—Mr. Presto does have an accent. He probably is Italian. But he's not a criminal. He runs a few stores and owns a bar on Prince Street and protects several other stores."

"Aha! So that's his game."

"He's a very nice man to me. Oh, and he does work with those Italian funeral homes."

Theodore was shocked that Elliott already knew so much about Presto's life.

Theodore worried for Elliott's safety—and for his own.

He decided that Elliott must see a dentist to straighten his teeth and whiten them, if possible. On the one hand he didn't want to render the boy even more desirable, but on the other he longed to remove every trace of Elliott's neglected child-hood.

Recently he'd dressed the boy at Lord and Taylor's. They'd visited the store, tried out the huge new hydraulic elevator (big as a brownstone living room), even seated themselves on the upholstered banquette as the room glided smoothly upward. The boy had been thrilled and a bit confused by the glare of the gas lamps on the main floor, many of them clustered densely together in one room designed to reproduce the harsh light at the new Metropolitan Opera so that ladies might judge how their gowns would appear there. A young woman who looked like an anarchist with her pince-nez, bun, and severe shirtwaist played the grand piano as customers spread out among the glass counters manned by clerks in flawlessly tailored suits. "That's the 'Marche Slav,' " Theodore had mentioned. "She's playing a piece by Tchaikovsky called the 'Marche Slav.' "

They bought a ready-made blue suit, two shirts, two ties, a gold tie pin, a change of baggy white underwear. Most of the men were buying fabric to be tailored later, but there were a few ready-made outfits available.

That evening Elliott modeled the underwear for Theodore, who loved the way the elasticized band crimped his thimble-thick waist, and his big hooded penis came poking out through the pearl-buttoned flies like a hand puppet surging up through the drawn curtains.

"If I correct your speech," Theodore said, "it's only so that you can rise in the world. The way you speak naturally doesn't bother me; in fact I like it, but I want you to bear no possible stigma. For instance, you must learn to moderate your tones. Sometimes your laugh is strident, and most of the time you mumble and are incomprehensible. You must speak clearly and audibly but never loudly."

The following Saturday Theodore accompanied Elliott to the Bronx. He had to make up a story to explain to Christine his absence during the weekend. He told Elliott he wanted to see how the small clay model was coming along but it was apparent to both of them that he was acting as a chaperone, which annoyed Elliott. Was the boy vexed because Theodore didn't trust him? Or did he hope to continue his flirtation with Mr. Presto?

Attilio frowned when he saw Theodore. "Here's the uncle, *lo zio*," he said in a matter-of-fact voice. "Now, my work is not yet ready to be inspected by the uncle. You will have to wait here in the *salotto* while the young nephew and me, we work. Too much talk can destroy the is-spiration, no?"

He conducted Theodore into a small room in the second atelier.

"Perhaps I could just have a glimpse—"

"No, no, no! Attilio Piccirilli does not work in this way!"

Theodore wondered if he was being kept out of the little locked room so that Mr. Presto might be admitted. He paced the sitting room and outside the French doors he saw a white carriage pull up drawn by a white horse. The horse was gigantic and when the small, compact driver flicked his reins over the horse's back, it reared up and paddled its massive hooves in the air. There was something appalling in the trained menace of those scissoring legs and the big albino head jerking from side to side, the bit foam-flecked. This was a killer's horse, Theodore thought. He'd never seen anything like it. Theodore stepped outside and approached Presto as he was descending from the box. He had thick black hair on the back of his hands. His face was handsome, or at least virile, but he'd obviously had a bad case of acne as an adolescent. He wasn't tall, but he was wiry, and he whistled when he walked, but quietly, as if he didn't want to share the melody with eavesdroppers.

Presto was bowed into the studio and, he presumed, into the locked workroom where Elliott was waiting, nude and vulnerable and standing on the base of a marble column.

Disgusted, Theodore scrawled a note to Elliott saying he was suddenly called away. He left the note with the studio assistant, the handsome one who could barely speak English and who now smiled and shrugged. He noticed that the assistant glanced nervously at the locked door.

Outside, Theodore took a closer look at the white horse. It stood three hands taller than any horse he'd ever seen, and it pulled restlessly back and forth in its traces as if it were too big and wild to do anything but rear up into the air and trample someone to death. He'd heard of killer horses like this one.

At lunchtime on Monday he went unannounced to the offices of Miss Smith, the private eye. He asked her to investigate Johnny Presto. He gave a description and told her he suspected Presto was allied with this new Black Hand organization that had killed the police chief in New Orleans a few years back and was attempting to "organize" Mulberry Street. "It's a good thing Teddy Roosevelt is our police chief," Theodore stated. "He won't put up with this kind of thing. Not that the people of New Orleans went along with it, either. When the Sicilians suspected of killing their police chief were found innocent by the jury, the people just broke into the jailhouse and shot them, or clubbed them to death. The king of Italy threatened to declare war on America and President Harrison had to pay an indemnity—"

"Yes, I know," Miss Smith said. "I, too, read the papers."

Later that day at six-thirty, Theodore went to Elliott's room. The boy was extremely agitated. "It's a fine thing," he said, "getting me mixed up with these Italians."

"What happened? Did Presto drive you home?"

"Did you see that horse of his? He says it's been trained to trample people to death."

"So he is a criminal?"

"No, he owns a bar, I told you."

"He could still be a criminal."

"He brags that store owners hire him to protect them from the real criminals. He laughed and used an Italian word, *pizzu*—"

"Sicilian. It's a Sicilian word. It means a piece of the action."

"And kidnapping. Not him, but he knows guys who kidnap children and even adults, for money."

"He told you all that?"

"Yes."

"Why would he do that?" Theodore asked.

"To frighten me, I guess. He wants me to be his . . . boy."

"He said that? His 'boy'?"

"Yes, he said, 'I want you to be my boy.' "

Theodore swallowed, "And what did you say?"

"I didn't want to say no. I was afraid to say no. And I don't want him to hurt you."

"How could he hurt me?"

"Blackmail."

"What are his terms?"

"He wants me to stop seeing you. He's very jealous."

Theodore felt everything was rushing forward. "And are you attracted to him?"

"That's the problem," Elliott said. "You're jealous, too."

Theodore pictured the white horse rearing back, its huge ironclad feet climbing into the air, the flecks of foam shaking from its bit. "But surely he could be . . . blackmailed, too. The Sicilians wouldn't be impressed if they thought their leader was in love with another man."

"I wouldn't try that one if I was—"

"Were."

"If I were you."

"What should I do?" Theodore said, "just walk away from everything we have?"

"I'm so nervous I can't sleep. There's a guy in a bowler hat with a short strong body and a pockmarked face who's staked out the door downstairs."

"I didn't notice him."

"I did. Oh, Ted, I don't feel safe here. The door's so flimsy. Anybody could break it down."

"Do you want to go back to your father's farm till this blows over?"

"No."

"I could send you somewhere, anywhere. You could hop on a train today and go to Atlanta. You don't know anyone in

Atlanta. I don't know anyone in Atlanta. I could send you some money every month."

"He'd find me. He'd kidnap you or your son, torture you till you told him where I was. I saw a play like that on Twenty-third Street."

"I'm sure you're exaggerating. There are other boys in New York. He would forget you. He wouldn't get away with it. We're not complete savages in this country. I could go to the police."

"And tell them what? That you and a gangster are both in love with the same guy?"

Theodore could tell from Elliott's eyes that he hadn't liked the idea that Johnny Presto might forget him.

Theodore hung his head. He felt that all along he'd been right to want to stop time or slow it down since no good could come from any change whatsoever.

He panicked, thinking how deep he had sunk. Of course he was vulnerable to blackmail, or violence, and yet even now it was hard for him to reconcile the simplicity (he wanted to say the innocence) of his feelings for Elliott with the labels that his enemies could affix.

The strange thing was that all these labels—fairy, pervert, androgyne—worked only when the "crime" in question was looked at from a great distance. Up close, at least, it didn't feel monstrous or criminal, and he honestly believed that other men, even fairly average middle-class men, might have responded the same way to Elliott's good looks and warm skin and availability had the boy happened to stumble into their arms instead of his.

"I'm just so sorry," Theodore said, "that I ever had the idea of arranging for you to pose for a statue. We were happy here alone in your room. We should've never stepped outside. At least I was happy—haven't you been happy, Elliott?"

"Yes, very." Elliott sat on Ted's knee but he didn't undress, and once he jumped up to his feet when he heard a floorboard creaking outside his door in the hall. He pretended he'd risen to adjust the curtain. "What's dangerous in life is going on seeing the same fellow," Elliott said. "Folks will let you get away with an occasional kiss and hug as long as you don't become attached to the same fellow, a particular fellow. Our fault was that we liked each other too much and wanted to have something together, like a father and son, or a man and his sweetheart."

On Tuesday at the bank Theodore received a note from Miss Smith the detective: "I'm unable to pursue this assignment. I've discovered that the gentleman in question is extremely dangerous and way out of my depth. I'm closing my books on this one and I suggest you do, too. Never mention his name to me again."

That evening it was so warm that some men were walking along with their jackets tossed over one shoulder. Pear trees up and down the side streets were seething with white blossom like bursting popcorn. Many of the passersby looked as if they had pushed a rock aside and emerged into the air and light after a long winter underground.

Theodore was working many hours at the bank and checked and rechecked his figures with the help of his assistant, but ten times a day discovered he hadn't really heard a remark someone had addressed to him. He woke every morning with a sinking feeling of doom. He was glad to return home too late to see the children, since he feared that he was about to destroy their lives—had already destroyed them.

Theodore ran into Mick on Union Square. "Hey, Mick," he said, touching the sleeve of the startled small boy, with his barrel chest, tiny hairless pink hands, and the long straight nose that almost reached his upper lip.

"Do I know you?" Mick asked loudly. "I don't thinks we's had the pleasure—"

"Mick, I'm Theodore. Elliott's friend. You took my pocket watch."

"I never stole no watch, nowhere at no time."

"And then you returned it very nicely, thank you very much." He put an arm around Mick's shoulder. "Elliott and I have a problem, a big problem."

"And his name is Johnny Presto," Mick said, pulling free of Theodore's embrace, as if he didn't want to know a marked man.

"So you've heard that already, have you?"

"Only because your little woman Ellen told me."

"Ellen. Oh, Elliott. That's what you call him, eh? Ellen? He told you?"

"Yes, but Mr. Presto is a well-known New York personality. He's the king of"—and here he lowered his voice—"you ever hear of the Black Hand?"

"Oh yes, so it's true." Theodore once again saw in his mind's eye the giant white horse rearing back and trampling the air.

"It's true, yeah, you betcha it's true."

"And has Elliott, or Ellen, told you how much he likes Mr. Presto? I suppose it's natural that any New York street kid would admire a real . . . leader like Mr. Presto."

"No," Mick said, frowning and slipping away into the crowd, "he don't never say nuttin' about Mr. Presto and you shouldna neither. Let's just say we never had this little talk."

Theodore felt shaken. That Mick knew of their plight frightened him even more. Theodore wished he hadn't said anything to Mick, who was capable of stirring up more trouble, of tipping off Johnny Presto just so he could make a buck or take on more importance.

When Theodore saw Elliott the next day, the boy looked exhausted. "This can't go on," Elliott said. "You have to stop coming here. You have to stop seeing me."

"But I can't stop," Theodore said. "Why do you say that? What's happened?"

"Johnny knows you're still coming here every day and he won't put up with it. 'You don't have no choice in this,' is what he said. 'You don't have no choice.' Ted, you have to forget me."

"How can I forget you?"

The next morning his assistant, Mr. Stallman, placed before him an envelope decorated with a small black hand in the upper-left corner, where the return address would normally be. It was like one of those printed hands designed to indicate an error in the street number.

Someone had laboriously printed the message: "Leave five thousand dollars in a plain envelope at ten a.m. tomorrow morning just inside the gate to your own house under the bush to the left. If it's not there, your wife and your employer will be told of your friendship with a certain young man named Elliott. If you go on seeing him something worse will happen to both you and yours."

Theodore took the letter out with him at lunch, tore it into tiny bits and threw it into the East River. The weather had turned freakishly cold and snow was falling, though it wasn't sticking. The flakes were large; it was almost impossible to distinguish between snowflakes and pear blossoms.

He waited until six o'clock, when no one else remained at the bank except two guards at the front door. All the clerks had gone home, Mr. Niedermayer had long since taken his leave, Mr. Stallman had lingered but at last been convinced he was no longer needed. Theodore could see that Stallman was confused; he knew perfectly well that there was no work to be done or that Theodore was so distracted he was incapable of performing even the smallest task. Tomorrow when the missing money would be detected, everyone would suspect him, and Mr. Stallman would be forced to give evidence against him.

There was no question of legitimately borrowing five thousand dollars. He had no collateral worth that much, nor did he make enough even to pay the interest on a loan of that size after his other expenses. He had no friends who could advance him such a huge sum and surely not at such short notice. Anyway, a blackmailer would never stop with the first payment.

He thought of jumping on a train himself and going to Atlanta, the very city he recommended to Elliott. But he would never be able to find a position there without letters of recommendation, and his reputation would be destroyed when he failed to pay off Presto and Mr. Niedermayer re-

ceived an anonymous letter about Elliott, the envelope decorated with a black hand.

If only he had insured his life for a large sum and could
arrange to die and make his death appear accidental, then
his insurance money could be paid to Christine (and a small
sum to Elliott). But now he didn't have the time to take out a
policy—and since the Panic and a rash of suicides, the insurance brokers had become much more cautious.

He knew all the details of the 1878 robbery of the Manhattan Savings Institution, but these robbers had planned
carefully for months, had conspirators directly in charge of
the vault—and, anyway, they had all been apprehended eventually. They had gotten away, at least temporarily, with
$2,747,700—but Theodore had no need of such a spectacular
sum. If he had had some advance notice he might have bribed
one of the guards to help him with the vault. In 1882 a bank
officer in Indiana had robbed his own institution of a large
sum—but again, that one had been apprehended, too. Theodore had just read of the treasurer of the bank in Gloucester,
Massachusetts, who'd killed himself when he was found
$40,000 short in his accounts.

Theodore didn't know what to do. The next morning he
entered the bank at nine, went to one of the tellers and said
he needed five thousand in cash for a private client. "Put a
memorandum in against me," Theodore said, as if this were
a standard bank procedure. He'd chosen a new teller, who
looked confused but who counted out the bills, then wrote
out a memorandum and asked Theodore to sign it.

"I'll bring it back later today, signed and dated and
stamped," Theodore said calmly.

Ten minutes later, at nine-twenty, he left the bank with

the money in an envelope. He took the elevated train and walked the few blocks to his house, hoping he wouldn't run into Christine.

Everything went well. He stepped into his own front yard, just a scrap of bush and lawn behind a freshly painted black wrought-iron fence. He pretended to be picking up a piece of litter but actually deposited the big manila bank envelope beside the bush on the left (left on entering the house? or left on leaving? the note hadn't been clear). He then slapped his forehead, miming that he'd forgotten something, in case any of the neighbors were spying on him. He looked at his old pocket watch from Paris, his *oignon*—it was ten.

He returned to the bank, hung up his hat and coat, sat beside his desk—and waited. He'd dressed very smartly that day in a plain blue serge suit, a blue cravat snugly tied at his low collar, and a cane, though he didn't need it and seldom walked with one. It was a beautiful, simple black malacca cane.

Maybe he'd have to wait till closing, when the assistant bank manager would ask the new clerk why he was coming up five thousand short.

At lunchtime Theodore walked down to the same spot on the East River. He went along Ann Street, past the National Park Bank and the Herald building. A month earlier he'd been inside this bank to look with placid, unmoved admiration at the central banking room with its fifty-foot ceiling. Now the bold scale of the white façade made him feel all the smaller and weaker. He thought of himself as a stray inhabiting the financial district, a noble marble city in which every inch of ground was coveted and contested, in which temples crowded each other just as they did in the ancient Forum of Rome. He was a Forum cat.

When he came to the water he tore the memorandum for $5,000 into tiny pieces. Once it was thoroughly shredded he cast it into the wind, which carried it over the rushing waves. He wanted to look over his shoulder to verify if anyone had seen him, but he was afraid of appearing guilty or suspect.

He went back to the bank without eating. The new clerk whose till he'd robbed tried to catch his eye and even called out, "Mr. Koch!" But Theodore avoided looking his way, even frowned, as if he'd heard but thought the clerk presumptuous. The poor fellow needed the signed memorandum, of course, to explain the deficit in his till.

As Theodore sat at his desk a formal feeling settled over him, as one must feel before being executed. One is still installed in the flow of time and one must breathe, swallow, look up, look down, loosen one's collar and the blue cravat with a finger, but all these motions are symbolic, and at the same time one has already entered eternity. He wasn't dead yet but he'd triggered the machinery that would lead to his downfall; he could already hear the gears shifting, the wheels turning, the product approaching. For the moment he was still the respected vice president of a New York bank, but by the end of the workday he'd be a criminal, possibly a prisoner in chains.

He thought about death and dying. All his life he'd joked around about death, as if he could put it off indefinitely by thinking about it, as if Orchus, the hairy, bearded giant who ruled the underworld, might be willing to substitute the burnt offering of one's fear, of one's jokes, of one's obsessive contemplation, for the pitiful reality of one's actual life.

As he sat there in his blue serge suit and his soft-collared shirt (how he hated detachable celluloid collars, which so many of the clerks changed every day but wore with shirts they hadn't washed in three days) he thought that now he might die, should die. He couldn't bear to see the horror and shame in Christine's eyes when she discovered that her husband was a thief and a fairy. If the milkman left one quart instead of two every other day Christine could scarcely cope with the disaster; how would she deal with a real tragedy?

Well enough, he thought. She was strong. She had lost her first husband. Now she could always return to Albany with the children and live with her mother. Maybe she'd change her name as Oscar Wilde's wife and children had. Holland—wasn't that the name Wilde's wife used? Her maiden name?

It might be consoling for some people to believe in the afterlife, but Theodore was happy it was nothing but a hoax to reward the downtrodden and scare the wicked. In fact any kind of afterlife—even the sort of feeble flicker of bored awareness in a dim no-man's-land that he could almost believe in—seemed childish to him. How absurd that the world should be constructed to reward and punish a particular brand of vertebrates. Every other man-centered and man-serving theory had been disproved by science—the Creation, the Garden of Eden, the flat world, the world as the center and principal stage in the whole universe, the shortness of history, the Flood that had engulfed everything. Darwin and the geologists and physicists had disproved all that, replacing a tight little claustrophobic world with a huge, ancient, and indifferent universe. So why would the afterlife, that most far-fetched of all tales, be the one belief to survive the harrowing of science? We see that the sun rises every day but we know it doesn't. We pretend to believe it rises unless we are being very serious and scientific. How much stranger that we would credit such a useful bit of flummery as the afterlife—and believe in it with no evidence whatsoever: none. Anyway, he wanted to be swallowed by oblivion; if there were an afterlife he'd be in hell.

Theodore had a philosophical turn of mind but he seldom let himself go this far, dig this deep. He was good at putting off difficult realizations. But now he sat as calm as a Buddha at his desk, though little flickers of anguish coursed through him from time to time.

He should have a plan. He should rehearse what he was going to say to Mr. Niedermayer. To Christine. He should work out a detailed, comprehensive libretto, with alternative arguments depending on the tack he or she took.

But then a philosophical sort of lethargy came over him; there were too many variables to control.

And maybe a total loss of control was what he'd always covertly been longing for. He felt as if he were a metal sign, half-rusted, creaking as it swung back and forth in the wind.

He could see Mr. Stallman tiptoeing around outside his office, wondering exactly what was happening. He'd registered Theodore's demotion back to current accounts with a muted show of sympathy. That sort of shift in the delicately weighted balance of power at the bank occurred rather often—not surprising, given how absentminded, even troubled, Mr. Koch was these days, Stallman must be thinking.

But now—well, now things seemed truly troubling, deeply troubling. Mr. Koch was all dressed up, he appeared to be half-drugged on grief or fear or gin; he hadn't signed any of the forms that had been placed before him; he merely sat there with his big-knuckled hands folded in front of him on the blotter. And at three the new teller had come by, looking timid and frightened, but Mr. Koch hadn't responded to his knock on the door. The man, Mr. Grey, had walked off, shrugging and whispering something to himself.

Theodore left the bank at five and walked slowly to Elliott's building. The fat-faced thug in the bowler hat had staked out the front door. Upstairs, as soon as Theodore knocked, Elliott came flying out of the room, fully dressed, and hurried Theodore down the stairs. Once they were half a block away (Theodore looked back and saw that the thug was following them), Elliott whispered, "I was scared you'd come by. We're both in trouble. Today I saw Johnny Presto at noon—"

"You did?" Theodore asked, astonished in a childlike way (in the manner of the child who says, "It can't be teatime, I haven't had my nap yet"). Theodore said, "You never see him at noon. You saw him? Here?"

"Yes yes *yes*!" Elliott hissed. "I see him often, whenever he wants, but the point is that today he laughed and told me he blackmailed you and made you steal five thousand dollars from your bank—"

Oh, Theodore thought, idiotically relieved: so he found my envelope. "He told you that?"

"Yes yes *yes*!" Elliott repeated, seething with impatience. "I got so angry with him for putting you through all that"— and here Elliott stopped and touched Theodore's sleeve—"for ruining your life, that I pushed him away and told him he was an evil man. I told him that you'd been good to me and that he couldn't just strike out against everyone in my life."

Theodore's heart pounded because he realized what he was overhearing was an account of a lovers' quarrel. Elliott loved Presto, even if he, Theodore, was still "in his life." Theodore pictured Elliott in Presto's arms.

And suddenly Theodore realized how *young* Elliott was, and though youth might be a magical coronation that happens to people, to everyone, but only for a moment, and that to be with that person in the moment he was wearing the crown could be a privilege, nevertheless Elliott's remarks reminded Theodore that youth is also attended by silliness and a vacillating immaturity.

Theodore suddenly stumbled, as if someone had punched him in the stomach, with the realization that he'd destroyed Christine and lost her all because of an infatuation with a kid incapable of understanding what was taking place in their lives, and how much it mattered.

FOURTEEN

WHEN STEPHEN AWOKE AGAIN IT WAS LATE, LATE BUT Cora, looking immense and bloated in her skirt stretched taut by her open, sagging knees, was still slumped down in her chair, snoring softly, even elegantly, one might say.

He glanced down and saw that his sheet was stained yellow. He must have pissed himself. He started to cry. So it's come to this, he thought. He'd gone back to infancy and incontinence—with this difference: an infant has everything ahead of him and a loud tam-tam is beating in his heart with anticipation, whereas he, Stephen, felt the rhythm slowing into a valedictory murmur.

He was so ashamed of himself.

Cora woke up suddenly and said, "Say, what's wrong, Duke?" Her thick hand pawed at her hair, which was sticking up where she had slept on it. "You're crying, my Mouse. What's wrong?" And then, out of her fabulous spirit of inconsequence, "Do you want me to find Spongie? Would that cheer you up—a visit from our doggy-boy?"

"No," he whispered, "no Spongie."

Now Cora was standing unsteadily, her skirt somehow twisted and not on right, her face puffy. She looked down and saw the urine-soaked sheet. "Here," she said, "let's change you and get you nice and clean." She pulled off the sheet and began to tug at his pajamas. "Now, you've got to let me put your pistol somewhere, no need for a big Colt, you foolish boy, when your Cora is freshening up. There, I'll put the pistol just here, I know how you love it, you'll have it back in a minute."

"I'm glad you're doing this and not one of the nurses. I'm so ashamed."

"Ashamed?" Cora croaked, apparently genuinely surprised. "Why on earth? It's just the poor body, Stevie, that's failing. But your spirit, your immortal spirit, is as strong and rambunctious as ever. And I do think it's immortal, despite what your Mr. Koch might be thinking. There now, lift up, I'm sliding these pants off—what's a wife for if not to hose down her husband when he needs it?"

She clucked and chuckled and Stephen felt relieved by her vulgarity and sweetness. He asked her, "Did I fall asleep while dictating? Were you able to get it all down?"

"You were whispering so faintly that I had to bend closer and closer to you and when one of the girls came in and clattered around I'm afraid I was rather violent shushing her and packing her off."

She was washing his genitals and upper legs and stomach with a cool cloth. He thought of himself as a baby being changed, but now that didn't feel shameful. It felt good. He liked it that Cora knew men's bodies so well and was such a regular fellow herself.

He remembered a picture of himself as a little kid in a sailor suit all splattered with mud. At the time he feared his mother would think he was just making more work for her, but she'd decided it was "adorable" and she'd urged someone with a camera to photograph him, which he disliked submitting to. His cold white anger is clearly visible on his mud-splattered face.

"What do you think of the new pages?"

Cora laughed as she jostled him into fresh pajama bottoms. "It's certainly a bizarre book and not really in your vein, what with the perverts and the criminals and the larceny and the death threats."

Stephen said, "Well, it's not that far from some of my journalism. Do you remember that piece I wrote called 'An Experiment in Misery'?"

"Yes. That's the Bowery vagrants, right?"

"Well? See?"

"Not exactly. But I like it, though it feels like being in a slowly sinking ship in the middle of the ocean."

"Do you think it's plausible? That a man who likes boys—Huneker says there are lots of them—would act that way? Feel those things?"

"It's very real and touching."

She wasn't lying just to cheer him up—Stevie was convinced she was being honest. You could always count on Cora to tell the truth.

"I just keep wondering if you're making it all up, or if you're basing it on something real, on real people."

"Hell, I never knew those people. I'm making it up. Though of course I knew Elliott fairly well." Oh, botheration, Stephen thought, this is where she's revealing that she's a woman after all, the personal slant. Women always assume a writer (or anyone, for that matter) never utters a word except out of tenderness or spite or self-interest. For women pure fiction doesn't exist; they can't believe in it, though quite a few do a good job writing it.

"I know you're inventing it all," Cora said. "And that's what proves your genius. But I keep wondering if Theodore's feelings for Christine—love and respect—aren't a bit like your feelings for me?"

Stevie reached out a hand toward his pistol, which Cora returned to him. "I do respect you and love you but you're a lot more interesting than Christine, and I hope to God that I have more verve and sap than poor old Theodore." He placed the pistol next to his scrawny thigh; he could feel the cold metal through his pajamas. "But I see what you mean. Of course, I don't permit myself to think about my own life when I'm writing. That's a superstition of mine. I'm certainly drawing on it, but it can only hurt to focus on it. Yes, but I see what you mean."

"If I'm Christine," Cora said, with a crafty look in her eye, crafty and vulnerable, "then who is Elliott to you? What woman?"

"Are you talking about Lily? Do you mean Lily?" Stephen asked, somewhat irritated. "Why would I base a boy on"—he almost said the great love of my life, but he modified it to—"on a married woman whom I once liked a lot?"

"Well, he's not just any boy, and Lily is not just any married woman. You were in love with her—in love with an unrequited love, just as Theodore is in love with Elliott."

Stephen felt offended by the comparison, though he did like being the center of Cora's attention, which made him feel important again. He wasn't just a dying man. He had a life, he could choose one woman over another, he was still a player on the team.

But he didn't even like the sound of Lily's name in Cora's mouth. And wasn't it absurd that all this petty jealousy should be aired now, so close to the end? He'd be dead in a day or two and Cora was still probing his poor, failing heart. Big, silly, awkward Cora with her bawdy house manners.

"First of all, Elliott is an adolescent boy, not an elegant married woman. And Theodore's tragedy, if there is one, is not that Elliott doesn't love him, for their love is obviously reciprocal. No, it's that . . . ," but suddenly a great weariness came over him and Stephen couldn't remember what he wanted to say. He closed his eyelids but they brought no relief to his burning eyes. His eyelids scratched at his eyes. Maybe he'd pissed out the last drop of moisture in his entire body. Dry. Everything in him was dry.

He could sense that he'd ruffled Cora's feathers and he reached out to pat her hand, though it cost him dear.

During the trip to Badenweiler, Stephen felt he was dead, though death, as it turned out, was a painful, humiliating state and not at all the eventless peace he'd hoped for. He was completely incontinent now and if he drank some milk or even water he vomited it or urinated it almost immediately. He had no desires at all—for food, for love, for survival. He wanted nothing but unconsciousness, and that he'd have soon enough. Oh, and he did want to finish his book.

He knew they were going up and up even before Cora said, "The Baedeker says we're on the northwest slope of Blauen Mountain. We're fourteen hundred feet above sea level. We're in a triangle between Switzerland, France, and Germany."

His last sense of self clung to the idea of being a good sport. He wanted to smile and laugh and be gallant in the face of death, but even gallantry seemed to him now only a way of hamming it up. He'd devised a few books as a bird might build a nest out of straw, foil, and the discarded collar button, and with any luck they'd outlast him by a decade or two, but authorship, reputation, friendship, and the few scratches one might have made on the papyrus—well, it all seemed friable and empty now, the merest exercise in vanity. And yet.

The house where he would be lodged in Badenweiler looked like the clock chalet a cuckoo pops out of—tall and narrow and outfitted with deep sun balconies and a sloping roof and intricately carved wooden shutters and doors. It belonged to someone who rented it out to the clinic.

Stephen was carried up through dim rooms that smelled of beeswax and a sour institutional disinfectant. All the shutters were closed. He could see nothing but the faint gleam of the furniture and floors. Leaning against a far wall was an immense mirror in a wood frame, curved at the corners. In the gloom it was a silver blur, the visual equivalent to a hushed chord played by all the strings.

The men who were carrying his stretcher were breathing heavily; he suspected them of wearing wide suspenders and lederhosen but he didn't have the strength to raise his head to verify or disprove his supposition. They were talking with each other in German in preternaturally deep voices; he wondered if German men from an early age on trained their voices to hit the bass register.

The windows upstairs were thrown open on a pulsing high rectangle of light and green leaves. Beyond could be seen the white blur of the Alps. He was very gently transferred by these two deep-voiced men onto a big soft bed. He glanced up to see the perspiring face of one of them, who needed a shave and whose whiskers were beginning to grow in gray, silver almost, against the dark-red flush of a beer-drinking peasant's face (though now he was surely inventing people to suit his preconceptions). Gentle as they were they still managed to hurt him. He thought that where their hands touched and lifted him there would be wide finger-shaped bruises in an hour.

The house felt more foreign than any place he'd ever been. The vivid pink geraniums in the window boxes, the cream-colored hand-knit throw at the end of the bed, the big-bottomed body of the uniformed *Schwester* who'd be nursing him—everything felt alien yet deeply convinced of its own authority, a parallel existence, as if he were already dead and had entered death's tall, narrow house.

The doctor came, a man in his mid-thirties who was obviously tubercular himself. His cheeks were sunken and his body as thin as a blade. The minute he saw Crane he threw up his hands in an angry gesture of impatience. "This man—why did you bring him here?" he asked Cora in English but with a strong German accent. "All for nothing. He will be dead in a few hours."

"Please," Cora said, bursting into tears and clutching the black braid of her fitted jacket. "Please, can't you see he can hear us, that he's alive and listening?"

"There is nothing I can do," the doctor said with the harshness of a man who is naturally sensitive but must be frank. Stephen looked at him and saw young eyes behind round glasses, a big beard, already beginning to gray, the hollow cheeks, worry lines as deep as scars and an overly prominent forehead, as if an ostrich egg were pressing through. He hoped the doctor himself would die soon, coughing his lungs out—no, he didn't. Emend that.

In a softer voice, the doctor asked, "Can you hear me?" Bending close to his face so that Stephen could smell the caraway-seed cheese he must have eaten for lunch, or would it have been breakfast?

"Yes," Stephen whispered.

"I'm so sorry you are in such pain," the doctor said with a mournful ring that sounded genuine. "We will do everything to make you comfortable."

Cora, who'd collected herself now, said, "A London specialist was of the opinion that only one lung had been affected. That if he could just—"

"Frau Crane," Dr. Fraenkel said, "just look at your husband. He may hemorrhage at any moment and die. It is all over."

"Why are you so cruel?" Cora wailed, sinking into a chair.

"I'm realist," the doctor said. "Why is this filthy dog here?"

Stephen could hear Spongie pattering about at the foot of the bed on the hardwood floor. "It's Mr. Crane's dog, his beloved Spongie," Cora said, tears in her voice.

"Mrs. Crane, you should repose yourself now, after your long voyage. *Schwester*, show her into her room."

"No," Stephen whispered.

"What is that?" the doctor asked, surprised, and even offended.

"Here," Stephen said. "I want her here."

"Would you like an injection of morphine, Herr Crane?" The doctor was already rolling back Stephen's sleeve.

"No, not now. I have things to tell Mrs. Crane."

"Very well. I'll return this evening. Don't let him get cold, *Schwester*. You must close the window in an hour. Maybe some bouillon now. I hope you are comfortable here in the Villa Eberhardt, Herr und Frau Crane. The street here, Luisenstrasse, is very quiet. The air in our town is very pure. I came to this town originally for my own health, and it is so *schön* that I stayed."

Soon everyone was gone, even Spongie. Stephen was alone with Cora. She moistened his lips with a wet washcloth, which fitted over her hand like a glove. His whole body ached, though it felt so insubstantial—even to him—what was left to ache? He tried not to cough for he feared he might cough out his last lifeblood. The tired-looking doctor, the realist, had said he might hemorrhage in an hour or two and die.

"Cora?"

"Yes?"

"Do you have the strength?"

She jumped up, though he knew she had a tricky ticker and shouldn't overstrain herself. "Of course!"

But what was this whole exhausting, expensive trip if not a strain? Even if she only hastened his death, as the realist was suggesting, he didn't mind. Better sooner than later. And the trip had been an adventure they'd shared. And for him, fortunately, it was strictly a one-way trip.

"—the strength to take dictation?"

"Yes," she said, scrambling for her notebook and pencils.

"There won't be time," he said, "to dictate the rest of the book. There will be two or three scenes to fill in—about five thousand words. You could ask James or Conrad or someone else, but someone skilled and open-minded."

"All right."

They could hear a dull, irregular clanging coming from somewhere near, but drifting. The source of the sound was moving like a church floating slowly downstream. Cora went to the window: "Cows," she said. "Cows with the biggest brass bells around their necks I've ever seen. I hope they won't be doing that all night."

"Cows don't—"

"What?"

"Cows don't graze at night."

"That sounds like an aria from that boring Mr. Handel's *Messiah*: 'Cows Don't Graze at Night.'"

Stephen smiled to indicate a laugh. "Come back, Cora. Come back, Imogene. Write this down."

She skipped back and sat down, knees together, with the mock penitence of a high-spirited schoolgirl, which really didn't suit her girth. She'd become much stouter in the last month—eating, no doubt, for two to sustain her for the long hours without sleep. "Yes sir," she said, saluting playfully.

"There should be a bit of running narrative. When Elliott scolds Presto for blackmailing Theodore, Presto becomes angry and vengeful. He sends an anonymous note to Mr. Niedermayer, telling him that Theodore Koch stole five thousand dollars out of the till to pay off a blackmailer. He even tells Niedermayer that Koch is in the thrall of a boy prostitute. Niedermayer fires Koch, of course, and this scene between Niedermayer and Koch should be given in full with dialogue back and forth."

"Does Niedermayer turn Theodore in to the police?"

"No," Stephen said. "No, he likes Theodore and cannot forget Theodore's seventeen years of faithful service. But he does say, 'It's as if I never knew you at all, Koch. You're not the man I thought you were. This . . . *crime*, and I don't mean the theft, has proved to me we never know the heart of another man—' No, no, soften that. Niedermayer wouldn't talk about the heart. Maybe Niedermayer should go back to calling him Mr. Koch. Anyway, Niedermayer promises not to press charges if Mr. Koch can pay back the stolen money within two months. Which moves old Theodore to tears he has to hide. Henry James will know how to subtle-ize all this, but don't let him cobweb it out of existence."

"I won't," Cora said, a mixture of fear and bravery in her eyes.

"Then the statue, fatally, the nude statue of Elliott, is delivered to Theodore's house. Theodore, of course, doesn't have the money to pay what's *due*, the second and final installment. He sends a polite note to Piccirilli to that effect, and the sculptor writes back a menacing letter that alludes to his criminal connections, but something veiled that couldn't be taken to court."

"How does Christine react to the statue? Does she know—"

"She knows right away it's obscene. It's too realistic. It's not of a noble athlete or a Greek god or a laughing faun. She can see from the sad eyes and modern, neat part in the hair and the tight, compact body, the pelvis tilted toward the viewer—she can see it's a portrait of someone she or her husband might know, the butcher boy or telegraph boy, say, or even a poor relation, because the boy is poor, that's obvious, not innocent or babyish like their son but totally disabused and, well—not cringing but unsurprised by any nasty blow fate might deal him."

"Does she say anything?"

"She orders Theodore to remove the statue right away. He doesn't know where to take it—certainly not to Elliott's room right under the nose of the thug with the bowler hat. Elliott suggests the androgyne, who agrees to take it. In fact she or he is thrilled to have a nude statue of a boy in her salon. Two movers with a horse and van convey the statue, covered with a sheet, to the androgyne's apartment on the East Side. Jennie June loves it and squeals with delight. The only problem is that Piccirilli has been waiting to sand away the black dots that cover the statue, the points, until after he receives the final payment. The statue looks as if a very pale young man has the pox—in any event it's an ominous sign."

"Where does Theodore get money to live on?" This was obviously a matter close to Cora's heart.

"He still has his last salary paycheck but in a week or two it'll run out. Elliott is terrified now. He knows how violent Presto is. Poor Theodore has nowhere to go. He doesn't want Christine to see him loitering about on a park bench. And he hasn't the money to sit all day even in a cheap café. He stays in Elliott's room, but the boy knows it's only a matter of days before Presto puts an end to these visits."

"Poor Theodore," Cora whispered. "Why doesn't Presto move Elliott out?"

Stephen licked his thin lips. Cora rose to moisten them gently with a sip of water. "Suddenly," Stephen whispered, "Presto demands that Elliott leave the very next day with him on an ocean liner bound for Italy. But Elliott doesn't show up at the dock. Furious, Presto disembarks."

"Oh, heaven help us," Cora said.

"That night Elliott's house burns down. Mick rings Theodore's bell at his family's home on Sixteenth Street in the middle of the night. Luckily Theodore hears the first bell before anyone else hears it. He has been awake, sitting in the drawing room. Mick says angrily, 'Now look what you've done, you worthless shit. Elliott's building burned down—it's been gutted. Come quickly.' "

"Burned?" Cora exclaimed. "Does Elliott die?"

"Tell James he can take some of those beautiful descriptions I wrote about fire in 'The Monster.' You remember when I talk about the twisting, glowing colors coiling like a serpent and dripping down onto the black man's face? It's a bravura passage. I always liked turning the horrid into something lovely."

He stopped to wonder how to do something similar now. He was propped up on his voluminous goose-down pillows and he was looking out at the distant Alps and listening to the cowbells, a sound that no American would ever be able to work out unless he actually saw the animals. Was there any way his gasps and sweats could be transformed by a gorgeous metaphor into organ bellows or stones exuding honey or trees secreting amber?

His thoughts were so vigorous that he felt like Tristan in the last act of Wagner's impossible opera which he'd seen once with Huneker during an excruciating evening at the Metropolitan. Madame Nordica had sung Isolde and Jean de Reszke was the elderly Tristan—the audience members, who paid five dollars each, were restless. Tristan is wounded, he wants to die, he almost does die but the wretched love philtre coursing in his veins keeps jolting him awake and filling him with longing. He wants to die but he can't.

Stephen suddenly had a horrible, Poe-like fear his aching lungs would deflate and stick together, his mouth would explode in a great red blossom of blood and he'd drown in it, his heart would stop—and his mind, imprisoned in this corpse, would go on churning even as he was buried, fully conscious. The thoughts sputtering through the last intact brain tissue. His veins were bursting with a philtre—a life philtre, a word philtre.

"What happens?" Cora asked.

No Isolde she, he thought (loving and pitying her). Though she's nearly as big now as a Wagnerian.

"Here, take this down," Stephen whispered.

THE PAINTED BOY (continued)

Frantic, Theodore threw on an overcoat and rushed down the deserted streets toward Elliott's building, trailed by an angry, hooting Mick, who kept yelling, "You bastard!" before reverting to noisy sobs and flailing at the air with his small hands. They encountered no one but a huge Clydesdale horse with its white blaze face and hairy legs and hooves as big as dinner plates, plodding noisily along and pulling a creaking cart and a dozing milkman. The full metal cans in the cart were packed in snugly and rattled dully against one another.

When they arrived at Elliott's address the building was smoldering like a giant smudge pot, a thick updraft of black smoke pouring out of it and stinking of naphtha. Splintered glass was shattered all over the sidewalk and street. In nearly every adjoining window neighbors were leaning out and calling down to friends and children on the pavement, which was slick with water. Many of those people milling around Theodore were half-dressed—and most of them seemed drunk. Why would so many people be staggering from drink at three in the morning?

A woman kept screaming, "Jack!" as she faced the crumbling, blackened façade. She called out with a sharp urgency toward the smoky ruins as if she seriously expected someone to answer her. "Jack!"

"Went up like a box of matches," a man behind Theodore said.

Three fire-patrol wagons, silvery and glowing dully in the dark, were parked uselessly and at odd angles in the street; the yellow gas lights in a dozen windows shone down on the impotent hoses unscrolled and abandoned on the sidewalk. The blinkered white horses stood motionless.

The atmosphere was of a backstage after the curtain has rung down on a big, noisy history play. People were still walking around, talking loudly, but the job was done and everyone was packing up and planning to go home.

The top three stories of the building no longer existed. They'd collapsed into the rubble below them. On the parlor floor, which was demolished by fire and fallen debris, Theodore could pick out, through the thick black smoke and the smashed-in windows, the leering clown face of a child's toy and the fire-strummed pages of a book, swollen by water to twice its normal size.

"Where is Elliott?" Theodore asked Mick.

A drunk old man standing next to them said, "Oh, he's dead. They're all dead. Everyone in the building is dead. They all died of the terrible heat or they were suffocated—no one escaped. They're all dead. Every last one of them. One poor woman came running out, shouting, but with no sound emerging, a human torch, no sound because her throat had already burned away. She crumpled at my feet like one of those flimsy paper wrappers you twist around an almond cookie . . ."

Theodore headed automatically over to Jennie June's apartment. She wasn't there but Theodore waited on the stoop until she returned, almost at dawn, with a drunk sailor in tow. Jennie looked terribly embarrassed; she obviously didn't want the sailor to escape, but she was kind enough to show the brute upstairs and then rush back down to the street. Theodore told her everything and wept against her big, cushiony body. He'd sought her out because he knew how much Elliott respected her—and on the off chance that Elliott had survived and fled to her apartment.

"OH, GOD," CORA SAID AS SHE WAS SCRIBBLING DOWN HIS words. "Poor Theodore."

As Stephen looked around, he realized that everything in the room had been carefully chosen. There were two chairs in metal of a supreme simplicity. Above the French doors hung a long narrow painting of little girls in crisp silhouette with fat stocking calves and thin thighs. One girl's shiny shoe, strapped above the ankle, dangled down out of the mauve border that was framing the picture.

Stephen began to dictate again. He felt as if he were some sort of sacred, oracular effigy, almost as if the recumbent stone statues of knights in medieval chapels could talk.

Theodore went into a terrible decline. He forced himself to rise every morning, shave and dress and leave the house. He would head over to the androgyne's apartment, sometimes walking the fifty blocks to kill time and save the three-cent fare.

Once he'd arrived at Jennie's place she'd give him a glass of lemonade or a cup of coffee and then discreetly leave him alone with the statue. Theodore would sit in a comfortable chair, which was covered with coffee lace, and weep as he looked at the statue. Sometimes the tears gathering in his half-closed eyes would well up and make the figure look as if it were moving, turning to one side or the other, and sometimes he'd sit on the other side of the room and contemplate this perfect body from another angle—a body at once so familiar, which his hands had explored day after day, and now so distant.

He thought he understood how the Romans must have felt when they deified their recently dead friends. He envied Hadrian's power to turn Antinoüs into a god, to crowd the whole empire with the likeness of the beautiful youth and to name a city after him beside the Nile, where he drowned, though Theodore knew, as intimately as he'd ever known anything, that Hadrian would have shattered every statue if he could have drawn the living man back onto his knee for even a moment.

Theodore never let himself touch the marble for he didn't want to know in his fingers that the illusion was false and the reality misleading. He saw the black spots on the marble as a symbol of Elliott's shame or unhappiness.

One day he came home to his own house (he had an alibi all ready to justify his early return) to discover Christine, pale and rigid, sitting in the salon all alone, her hat and cloak still on, her hands looking pale and *washed*, working and working in her lap as if she were wringing out rags. Her face was expressionless and her body upright, but her hands were working feverishly, almost as if she were making something.

Theodore sat down in his hat and overcoat.

After a long silence and the sound of a horse trotting past down Sixteenth Street, Christine said, in a dull voice, "I happened to be in the financial district today, in order to get my watch repaired, and I thought I'd surprise you at the bank and whisk you off to lunch. The clerk looked very unhappy and went to fetch Mr. Niedermayer, who called me into his office. You know what a big stomach he has, but he kept crossing and uncrossing those long skinny legs of his, and staring at a spot a foot above my head and a bit to the left."

"Did he—?"

"Yes, he told me you'd been dismissed. That you'd taken out a huge loan to repay the money you had stolen but that you'd already defaulted on the first payment."

"That's because I don't have a penny. We're ruined."

"He said that you were being blackmailed because of your *reputed*—he had the decency to say reputed—your reputed involvement with a person of dubious character."

"Who's dead. The same gangster who blackmailed me killed that person."

Christine pressed her fingertips to her temples and closed her eyes. It was as if she were miming a headache because it would be too cruel to cover her ears. Either way, it was clear she wanted no more information.

They sat in silence and listened to the grandfather clock in the hallway ring out the hour. It was three o'clock. The clock sounded poignant, not reassuring, because soon it would no longer belong to them.

"What shall we do?" Christine asked.

"I will find money somehow. Not in banking because I could never get a letter of recommendation. In all the world we have only seventy-five dollars left to our names."

"I'll dismiss the servants and do the cooking and laundry and cleaning myself," Christine said with an odd little jerk of her chin upward, a tic he'd never noticed before. "I'll dismiss them today." After another long silence, punctuated by the laughter of children running past on the sidewalk, she asked, "How will you earn money?"

He said, "Maybe we will move to Europe. I could ask my family for some money to get us started there. I don't know."

Maybe the hopelessness of their predicament only now impressed itself upon her. She questioned his ability to do anything right, she who had always trusted in his unassuming, mild-mannered reliability. That's what she had loved about him: his reliability. She began to cry.

It was obvious to Theodore that she wasn't used to crying, that she had no "style" of grief. That she was improvising her emotion in a blind, clumsy fashion. Little cries, very high-pitched, broke out of her in a strange, staccato fashion.

He went to his room and didn't emerge all evening. From his desk he could dimly hear the rites of his household—the children returning from school, the genteel ruckus of their snack, their giggling baths, their noisy, combative hours of homework. He could smell the tomato soup being heated for their supper. A bowl of it was placed on a tray in front of his door and someone rapped lightly to let him know it was there. He lapped at it with a weary, canine, posthumous feeling, just as a sick dog, eyes gelatinous with death, will lick its lips only if they have been moistened by its loving mistress.

The next morning there was a letter for Theodore, which Christine placed beside his bowl of porridge. She was doing the cooking and serving—apparently she'd already dismissed the servants. The scent of a strong perfume—Lily of the Valley?—arose from the heavy paper envelope on which his name had been written in a bold, feminine hand, all circles (even the dots over the *i*'s were circles). It was a note from the androgyne:

> I have good news. Elliott is alive though horribly burned. He doesn't want to see you. He'd rather leave you with your memories of him in all his glory, which he appreciates only now that he's lost it. Though if you want to see him, you'll find him chez moi.
>
> Yours faithfully,
> Jennie June

Theodore's veins began to pound so loudly in his right ear that he was afraid he'd go deaf or faint or have a heart attack.

He stood, bumped into a chair, got his foot caught in a silk scatter rug and nearly fell forward. No one was there to observe him. He heard a sound ushering from his own lips though it wasn't his usual voice: "Thank you, Lord, oh, thank you!" Which was absurd since his brain didn't believe in God, even if his entrails did. He thought, Elliott says he doesn't want to see me, but he must have been the one to give Jennie my address.

He rushed upstairs and gave himself a quick maid's bath, shaved with a razor he'd forgotten to strop and which nicked his neck and chin. With trembling hands he dabbed at the bloody spots with witch hazel and cotton wool. He rooted around for a styptic pencil but couldn't find one.

He dashed onto a trolley and stood in the crowded car. God had smiled on him. He'd sinned, and all of them had been punished, but now God had forgiven him. Now it was over . . .

Theodore wanted to duck into a church, buy candles and light them before every saint. How intelligent the Catholics had been to dream up so many gods and goddesses to worship; a great blessing required multiple prayers and offerings to a whole panoply of saints, especially to that one for lost causes—was it Saint Jude?

He didn't let himself think about the future. He'd trained his thoughts to veer away from it, to sense even the distant approach of the subject and to dart down some mental sidepath. But now, for the first time in months, the future, though still unthinkable, presented itself as a sunrise suffusing the horizon.

He would live! He wouldn't have to die, or, even worse,

live without Elliott. He loved the boy, not just his body. Elliott had been resurrected.

Only now, in his relief, did he acknowledge how crippled he'd been by his sense of responsibility for Elliott's death. He'd known in his guts (where it appeared so much of his thinking took place) that he'd killed the boy, and this knowledge had been the most intolerable of all his sufferings. He killed the boy he loved, the only person he had ever loved, and fate, with radical unfairness, had given him no chance to substitute his own life for Elliott's.

He was a modern Nebuchadnezzar; his sanity was being reignited after years in the wild and he suddenly found himself on all fours, his mouth full of needles.

He rushed up the stairs to Jennie's door and pounded merrily on it (should he have brought her a celebratory box of chocolates?).

She opened the door, her heavy body barely discernible through the layers of floating fabric, and held a finger to her lips. The room smelled not of the usual feminine scent, Lily of the Valley, but of something maritime and restorative, the fragrance of algae and burning sage. If he hadn't already realized Elliott was convalescing, this briny, smoky odor would have convinced him. Theodore counseled himself not to reveal any hint of surprise when he saw the boy's burned face and body for the first time.

They made their way back to the bedroom, which Theodore had never seen and which he now thought he was somehow violating, as if it were a maiden aunt's virginal chamber. The room was small, barely large enough for the double bed, which was a four-poster with a lace canopy.

In the dim light Theodore wondered if Elliott were really there or if a black puppy had been substituted for him, because Theodore caught a glimpse of something very black and shiny and small lolling from side to side.

And then, as Jennie withdrew almost breathlessly, Theodore's eyes adjusted to the dimness and he realized this black, charred, hairless thing was Elliott's head and face, but mostly under bandages which for some reason were stained a dark yellow. He had no proof that this ball of soot—featureless, small—could belong to (could *be*) Elliott, but he took its (*his*) identity on faith, since faith was what was most needed now. Theodore bit his fist. He suspected the algae smell was only masking the naphtha stink of burned flesh.

Was there a mind ticking inside this dented sphere, the burning wick leading up into the cannonball?

"OH, POOR ELLIOTT!" CORA EXCLAIMED.

Stephen couldn't turn his head to look at her but he could hear the tears in her voice. Was she crying for him or herself or for Elliott?

"Will he die?" Cora asked.

"No, because I saw him scarred but weaving through the crowds on Wall Street, selling his papers. I told you about that day when I saw him burned."

"Yes, but—" she said, interrupting herself, then continuing, "but you're talking about the real Elliott." She then composed herself but still sounded excited when she asked, "But in the story, *The Painted Boy*, does the character Elliott get better?"

"I don't know—I haven't written it yet. Yes, he does. Tell James

to write the scenes of Theodore sitting by his bed at Jennie's apartment day after day, week after week. "

"He gets better—but he's disfigured?"

"Elliott gets better, the bandages are removed, his face is unrec-
ognizable, his chest and one arm are covered with shiny waffles and
puckers of flesh—take all this down!"

"Oh . . . I'm sorry."

He could hear her scribbling dutifully. It was all for her own
good, a legacy for her. If she could get Henry James to fill in the
missing scenes toward the end, then she would have something
saleable.

He said, "There should be a scene in which Jennie leaves them
alone in the sitting room with the statue. She closes the curtains
and the door to the room and the two men caress each other while
both are looking at the marble boy."

Stephen turned his eyes toward the open door, where a youngster was scrubbing the floor. Crane thought he saw the statue
there, but as the living boy, naked, without the spots, intact and
laughing.

Simultaneously, he felt he was on some great battleship being
christened and launched. He could feel hawsers and guylines giving way as tons and tons of painted steel plunged into the surpris-
ingly warm ocean.

"What happens?" Cora cried. She was frantic to know how it
would all turn out. "What happens to Christine, the wife? What
about the wife and children? How have they lived without money?"

There was a scuffling and two big white-robed nurses smelling
of tar soap pulled her away from the lifeless body and the open
mouth, which was welling over with blood. Stephen's eyes were
open and fixed.

Cora was injected with something that calmed her. She couldn't quite believe, even in her tranquilized state, that the long, long struggle to keep her husband alive, a struggle so full of incident, of ups and downs, had at last ended in a bloody mouth and a cold, small, boneless hand.

When she awoke from a guilty sleep full of punctures and angry German voices and a nameless feeling of catastrophe, the body had been removed. Its absence made her frantic—maybe she could still revive him. In another way she wanted nothing more to do with it, this burnt-out hive from which all of Stephen's buzzing thoughts had swarmed. His body was a reproach to her; it told her she had failed. She'd been given a precious possession, but not to own, only to borrow, and she had let it drop from her hands. She'd been the clumsy peasant woman to whom the infant prince is confided for safekeeping and concealment, but she'd allowed him to be discovered and killed.

They'd changed Stephen's bed, and the blood-flecked sheets had been removed, as if a giant snow had fallen all day long on the place where he had lain.

That evening a nurse handed Cora a note from Henry James in which he'd enclosed fifty pounds. Since she knew through hearsay that he only paid seventy-five pounds a year for that lovely Lamb House in Rye, with its walled gardens and attractive reception rooms, she realized what a considerable outlay this represented for him. Poor bugger with his long, unreadable but distinguished books, he couldn't possibly earn much—and she broke down into a new lament for James and his feeble talent, and for Stephen and his great genius now that it had flown the coop. Those busybody nurses and the cold Jewish doctor had at least had the dignity to release Spongie from the cellar. In the twilight, so dim down here in the valley but still gleaming brilliantly on the snow-covered peaks in the distance, Spongie's sad eyes were dark as little plums.

Cora remembered the ridiculous quarantine England imposed on pets from abroad. She pulled herself together sufficiently to wire a friend in London who worked in the American Embassy, "God took Stephen at 11:05, make some arrangement for me to get the dog home."

A month later Cora was living in London, trying to find journalistic hackwork to pay her crushing bills. She'd arranged to have Stevie's body displayed in London in a glass coffin, and hundreds of friends and the merely curious had trooped past. After many telegrams to Stephen's brother, it had been decided that the sealed coffin would be returned to America for burial. Of course: Stephen was the most American of all writers. The remains were in transit.

By now, Cora had dictated the entire manuscript of *The Painted Boy* to an English woman who'd then typed it. They worked for three days, early to late, and the woman had demanded three pounds for the endeavor—which was robbery but necessary.

In the margins, Cora had clearly indicated the changes and additions she thought Mr. James should make. And she'd of course flagged the unwritten scenes that Stephen had left blank for him to fill in.

She was especially curious about how Mr. James thought that the book should end. Would Theodore live miserably ever after, divorced, embracing his "burnt offering to the gods" (she was proud of that poetic turn of phrase and thought it would tickle Mr. James)? But that would mean abandoning Christine and the children, though she supposed they could always change their last name, as Stevie said Mrs. Wilde had done. And Christine could return to her father's rectory in upstate New York. Poor woman, just imagine the boredom. Would the bank write off the loss, or hold Christine accountable forever after? Such questions of debt and legal action interested Cora, as Mr. James would easily understand.

She sent the typed copy and the only version of the actual manuscript (all of Cora's handwritten dictation notes) to Mr. James. She imagined he would be moved by what were literally Stephen's dying words. Hadn't Mr. James been just the least bit sweet on Stevie? And, in a postscriptum, she asked him if he could spare another twenty pounds.

A week went by, anxious days.

Then, at her rooms in London, she received an envelope of the best vellum paper, creamy and all but coroneted:

Dear Mrs. Crane,

Due to my own exigencies (considerable now that somehow, improbably, I've ended up with three servants attending to me: I've never been so much under the reign of the *petticoat*), I am disarmed financially and grieved to be unable to help you further. Nor am I able to receive you as a guest here at Lamb House, a genial idea you so gaily proposed, since my brother and his considerable brood are about to descend on me for a month.

As for the curious little text you sent me, I was of course mesmerized by the bizarre fancies that belabored our Stevie's dying brain. Who would've thought that he—or anyone we know!—could have developed such unwholesome thoughts. Truly *malsain!* And (to use my most condemning modifier) how *straightforward* he was in his procedure!

Never fear, I have quietly committed this embarrassment to the fireplace here at Rye. Not a word remains. Naturally, you and I both wanted to silence even the slightest rumor that such a dank inspiration ever besmirched our Stevie's genius, characteristically so sunny and virile. Never fear. Now his reputation is safe. We have protected it.

Yours faithfully,

Henry James

POSTFACE

This novel is my fantasia on real themes provided by history. Stephen Crane did in fact die in Bavaria after a period of living in Sussex. He was indeed working on *The O'Ruddy*, a minor work he left incomplete at his death, though someone else eventually finished it and published it (to no acclaim). Crane did live with Cora Crane, who presented herself to the world as Stephen's wife though in fact she could never locate her second husband to arrange the divorce that would have permitted her to marry Crane. She did in fact run a whorehouse in Jacksonville called Hotel de Dream, and after Stephen's death she did go back to Florida and open another bordello, this one called The Court. She had a weak heart and died ten years after Crane, in 1910, after overexerting herself helping push a stranger's car out of the sand. She does seem to have been "a good fellow."

As for the manuscript I call "The Painted Boy," everything about it appears to be uncertain (which makes it challenging mate-

rial for a novelist). According to Crane's friend the New York critic
James Gibbons Huneker:

> One night in April or May of 1894, I ran into Crane on Broadway and
> we started over to the Everett House together. I'd been at a theater with
> Saltur and was in evening dress. In the Square, a kid came up and begged
> from us. I was drunk enough to give him a quarter. He followed along and
> I saw that he was really soliciting. Crane was damned innocent about
> everything but women and didn't see what the boy's game was. We got to
> the Everett House and we could see that the kid was painted. He was very
> handsome—looked like a Rossetti angel—big violet eyes—probably full
> of belladonna—Crane was disgusted. Thought he'd vomit. Then he got
> interested. He took the kid in and fed him supper. Got him to talk. The
> kid had syphilis, of course—most of that type do—and wanted money
> to have himself treated. Crane rang up Irving Bacheller and borrowed fifty
> dollars.
>
> He pumped a mass of details out of the boy whose name was some-
> thing like Coolan and began a novel about a boy prostitute. I made him
> read A Rebours which he didn't like very much. Thought it stilted. The
> novel began with a scene in a railroad station. Probably the best passage of
> prose that Crane ever wrote. Boy from the country running off to see
> New York. He read the thing to Garland who was horrified and begged
> him to stop. I don't know that he ever finished the book. He was going to
> call it "Flowers of Asphalt."

There are lots of things wrong with this single piece of paper
found among the Thomas Beer Papers. As Paul Sorrentino and
Stanley Wertheim, the two leading Crane scholars, have pointed
out in *The Crane Log*, it seems unlikely that Crane and Bacheller
were well acquainted at this time, nor would Crane, given his own

poverty, have been able to borrow such a substantial sum from anyone, especially not to aid a total stranger. On another occasion Huneker told someone that Crane had begun "Flowers of Asphalt" in 1898, but at that time he was in Havana and certainly no longer innocent of New York street life.

Did he ever meet such a boy and start such a novel? Was it meant to be a companion piece to *Maggie, A Girl of the Streets*? If he did start it, did it really have such an ugly title? One suspicious fact is that a poem by a popular French bohemian writer of the period was called (the far more euphonious) "Fleurs de bithume." Subtitled "Petits poèmes parisiens," it was written by Emile Goudeau, and Huneker, who was up on all things French, might have known of this title and simply translated it. Crane had the odd fate of having two of the first people who wrote about him, Huneker and his first biographer, Thomas Beer, turn out to be fabulists of an exaggerated sort. Beer even made up documents wholesale that were supposedly from Crane's pen. The falsifications were discovered only in recent times. In fact Crane has yet to be the subject of the big authoritative biography he deserves, though Dr. Sorrentino is embarked on it. After editing Crane's letters, collaborating on the *Log*, and compiling in one hefty volume all the reminiscences of Crane written by his friends and acquaintances, Sorrentino has assembled all the elements necessary for the definitive biography.

Crane is one of the classic American authors of the nineteenth century, along with Hawthorne, Melville, Dickinson, Emerson, Thoreau, Whitman, and James, but in many ways he remains one of the most mysterious. Of course this very obscurity has provided me with the space necessary to invent. I have tried to imagine in this book what "Flowers of Asphalt" might have been like, though not one word of it is extant. How would a heterosexual man who had wide human sympathies, an affection for prostitutes, a keen, compassionate curiosity about the poor and downtrodden, a terminal disease—how would such a man have responded to male homosexuality if he was confronted with it? How would he have thought about it in an era when homosexuals themselves were groping for explanations of their proclivities?

ACKNOWLEDGMENTS

I was a fellow at the Dorothy and Lewis B. Cullman Center of the Forty-second Street library for nine months in 2005–6. I consulted several hundred books while at the library and spoke often to librarians, especially Warren Platt. I had to find out, with other people's generous assistance, everything from what Brede Place looked like in 1900 to the price of a life-size marble statue in the 1890s if sculpted by a mediocre artist of moderate fame. I am grateful to the Cullmans for the fellowship and to Princeton University for time off from teaching.

A former fellow, George Chauncey, the author of *Gay New York*, directed me toward glossaries of old gay slang. Paul Sorrentino generously read through the manuscript. And caught many mistakes. His work has been of paramount importance to me and to anyone who is studying Crane.

I also spoke on a daily basis to other fellows, in particular the American historian Kirk Swinehart, the New York architectural historian Rebecca Shanor, the biographer Andrew Meier, the

Hebrew scholar Ray Scheindlin, and the two Irish novelists Mary Morrissy and Joseph O'Connor. Jean Strouse, the director of the Cullman, was always quietly encouraging and welcoming—and an intellectual example to us all. Adriana Nova and Pamela Leo explained a hundred mysterious workings of the library to us. Paul LeClerc, the director of the library, was a wonderfully warm and nurturing presence.

My life companion, Michael Carroll, once again took good care of me and read every word of this book in several versions, though I alone am responsible for its faults. Patrick Merla gave me the benefit of a detailed reading of my book. I am grateful to our little band of writers for their precious counsel—Will Evans, Joyce Carol Oates (my muse), David McConnell, Keith McDermott, Sheila Kohler, and, of course, the dedicatee of this book, Patrick Ryan.

Finally, I want to thank my editors, Dan Halpern in New York and Michael Fishwick and Rosemary Davidson in London, as well as my American agent, Amanda Urban, and my British agent, Deborah Rogers.

B L O O M S B U R Y

BLOOMSBURY